Highlander's Return

Books by Emma Prince

The Sinclair Brothers Trilogy:
Highlander's Ransom (Book 1)
Highlander's Redemption (Book 2)
Highlander's Return (Bonus Novella, Book 2.5)
Highlander's Reckoning (Book 3)

Viking Lore Series:
Enthralled (Viking Lore, Book 1)
Book 2 coming late 2015!

Other Books:
Wish upon a Winter Solstice (A Highland Novella)

Highlander's Return

The Sinclair Brothers Trilogy

Book 2.5 (Bonus Novella)

By

Emma Prince

Highlander's Return
(The Sinclair Brothers Trilogy, Bonus Novella Book 2.5)

Copyright © 2014 by Emma Prince
Print Edition

All rights reserved. No part of this publication may be reproduced, distributed, or transmitted in any form or by any means, or stored in a database or retrieval system, without the prior written permission of the author except in the case of brief quotations embodied in critical articles and reviews.
For more information, contact emmaprincebooks@gmail.com.

This is a work of fiction. Names, characters, organizations, places, events, and incidents are the products of the author's imagination or are used fictitiously. Any resemblance to actual events or persons, living or dead, is entirely coincidental.

For Scott. Always.

Chapter One

Scottish Highlands
Late July, 1307

"Farewell!" Burke glanced one last time over his shoulder at his cousin Garrick and the English healer lass Jossalyn. Though he would miss their company, he also felt relieved to be out of their hair. It was obvious the two were in love—and that they snuck off to explore that love whenever they thought Burke wasn't paying attention.

Of course, he knew what they were up to, and what grew between them. He had experienced it himself. Although it was years ago, he would never forget the feeling of true and deep love blossoming for the first time.

You two had better be married the next time I see you. Burke's words to Garrick floated back into his mind as he nudged Laoch, his bay stallion, into a trot. He hoped his advice to his cousin sank in—Garrick could be stubborn and resistant to being told what to do, but it was plain as day that he and Jossalyn were meant to be together. She was the sister of Raef Warren, the Sinclair clan's greatest enemy, but that couldn't stop their love.

As expected, Garrick had bristled slightly at Burke's words. *You're not her father, Burke...*

Take the word of a man who regrets not being able to follow his own advice, he had replied.

Aye, Burke knew more than Garrick about love—and losing it.

Perhaps you can still find happiness... Garrick had eyed him closely as he spoke, and his voice held a note of sympathy. Perhaps Burke had said too much. He didn't want his cousin's pity. He had resigned himself years ago to the fact that he would never again experience the kind of perfect passion and deep connection he had felt with—

Meredith.

Meredith *Sutherland*.

Burke used her clan name like a knife, twisting it into his chest to remind himself yet again why he could never be with her.

Even though nearly ten years had passed, the pain was still sharp. He leaned into it so that he would remember not to get hurt like that again. He had been young and foolish to fall in love with a Sutherland. Everyone in the Highlands knew that the Sinclairs didn't get along with their neighbors to the southwest.

And "didn't get along" was an understatement.

Their clans' centuries-old blood feud still ran hot. If anything, Burke and Meredith's brief but intense encounter ten years ago had only made the simmering conflict heat to a near-boil again. Luckily, no blood had been drawn for decades, but that wouldn't have been the case if Burke and Meredith's plan to get married had worked.

He supposed he should feel grateful that they hadn't succeeded, that she had been married off to some Sutherland clansman, and that they had never done what both of their youth-fired bodies had longed for.

But he didn't feel grateful. Instead, the thought of Meredith Sutherland and their forced separation sat like a stone in his stomach.

Burke suppressed a sigh, despite the fact that he now rode alone through the forest a few hours west of Inverness. Even when he was completely alone, he always forced himself to maintain his composure when it came to thoughts of Meredith. If he let go of his vise-like grip on his self-control, even for just a moment, he wasn't sure if he would be able to regain it again.

He had forced himself to move on from Meredith, forced himself to forget the rich, dark waves of hair that smelled like roses, the deep brown eyes that swallowed him whole, the lush firmness of her body, the sweet smile made mischievous by the sprinkling of girlish freckles over her nose…

Hell, who was he fooling? The mere memory of

her stirred him more than the actual presence of other women he had encountered over the years. Nay, he would never forget her, no matter how hard he tried. But, he reminded himself for the thousandth time, he would never get to be with her again either. There was the true source of his pain: she haunted him still, but she might as well be dead to him, for he would never again know true happiness with her.

As the deep but familiar ache settled into his chest, he guided Laoch slightly westward. He had several long days of travel ahead of him before he reached Roslin Castle on Sinclair lands. The journey would only take a couple of days if he could travel in a straight line across northeast Scotland, but Sutherland lands stood between him and his destination.

His head whipped around at the sound of a snapping branch behind him. It was just the summer breeze, of course. Bloody hell, he was already jumpy at the mere thought of crossing Sutherland lands.

It wasn't wise for a man—a Sinclair, no less—to travel alone across Sutherland holdings. But haste was of the essence. He needed to reach Robert, his cousin and Laird of the Sinclairs, as quickly as possible to tell him the news.

Longshanks was dead.

Edward I, King of England, Hammer of the Scots, was dead.

Burke and Garrick had been sent by Laird Robert Sinclair and Robert the Bruce, the self-crowned King of

Scotland, to the Borderlands to gather information on the English army's movements. There were ever-loudening rumors of a mounting attack on Scotland coming from the Borderlands, and the more they could learn—covertly—the better.

The two of them had arrived at Dunbraes village nearly a month ago, keeping a low profile by passing themselves off as two traveling blacksmiths looking for work. The village, along with Dunbraes Castle, was held by Lord Raef Warren, the English bastard who had brought war and destruction to Sinclair lands in the battle at Roslin four years earlier.

Even though Warren had been away during their week-long mission, they had overheard plenty about the increasing activity of the English army in Dunbraes. But they never expected to hear the town crier announcing not only Lord Warren's return to Dunbraes, but also the news of Longshanks's death.

They had been forced to fight their way out of Dunbraes and travel hard through the Scottish wilderness—with a new travel companion as well. Jossalyn Williams, the shy but strong-willed English healer lass at whom Garrick couldn't stop staring, was actually Jossalyn *Warren*, Raef Warren's sister. Blessedly, she had been able to treat a wound in Burke's leg that might have otherwise killed him.

He unconsciously rubbed the now-closed wound on his right thigh at the memory as he rode northward. The skin was still pink and new, and he'd have a hell of a scar, but at least he was alive—thanks to Jossalyn. Despite the fact that she was the sister of their enemy, Burke couldn't hold Garrick's love of the lass against him—she was strong, smart, and beautiful. Of course, she didn't stir him the way that—

Nay, he wouldn't think of it—of *her*—again. He had a mission to complete. He had to stay focused.

Garrick and Jossalyn were headed toward Robert the Bruce's secret rebel headquarters outside Inverness. Once there, the two of them could focus on aiding the rebellion side by side. And if Garrick heeded Burke's warning, they would see to getting married soon, too.

Burke, on the other hand, needed to report back to his Laird and closest confidante, Robert Sinclair. As Robert's right-hand man, Burke was loyal to him to the death. Burke had bristled at first at being sent on this mission to the Borderlands with Robert's younger brother. His place was at Robert's side—especially since Robert's new wife, Alwin, was with child. Robert was frequently, and understandably, distracted these days.

Garrick hadn't exactly been excited to travel to the Borderlands with Burke either, but neither one of them could defy both their Laird and their King. Garrick was taking care of half their mission by informing the Bruce of all they had learned. The other half of the mission—reporting back to Laird Robert Sinclair—fell to Burke.

He had to get back to Roslin to tell Robert that Longshanks was dead, that Warren had pursued them into Scotland, and that the English army was stirring in the Borderlands. His news could affect the entire country. It could mean either the start or the end of the Scottish war for independence from England.

That thought brought him back to the gravity of the situation he was in. Sutherlands be damned. Burke couldn't waste two days skirting their lands because of an ancient blood feud. The fate of Scotland hung in the balance. He would just have to cross their holdings.

He would have to ride carefully, even more so than the last week and half as he, Garrick, and Jossalyn had traveled north through Scotland. He was alone now, with no one to watch his back. And if he didn't reach Robert and deliver his news as fast as possible, he would have failed—failed his mission, his Laird, and his country.

He couldn't let that happen.

"Come on, *Hero*," he said, patting Laoch's neck. He guided the bay stallion to the northeast and spurred him on, straight toward Sutherland lands.

Chapter Two

Chisolm Sutherland was dead.

Meredith had to remind herself of this every few hours, for although it had been several weeks since her husband had passed away in their bedchamber, she still slunk through Brora Tower as if it weren't her home.

In fact, Brora was more hers than it had ever been Chisolm's, and yet her husband had made her feel like a guest—nay, an intruder—in her childhood home.

But Chisolm Sutherland was dead now, she reminded herself yet again. She straightened her spine as she climbed from the top floor of rooms to the roof of the tower house. She no longer had to be afraid of his harshness, his cold dismissal, or his groping, demanding hands.

The warm, late-summer sun touched first her head and then her shoulders and back as she climbed up the ladder and onto the flat parapet that ringed the tower's roof. The air was still and heavy with the warm scent of the surrounding green hills. She could even catch a faint whiff of salt in the air coming from the North Sea off to the east. She inhaled deeply, letting the fresh air and sunshine seep into her and lift the shroud of despondency that seemed to be ever-present of late.

Nay, not just of late. If she told herself the truth, which she could now that she was a widow, the darkness had closed in on her the day she was married, nearly ten years ago, to Chisolm.

It had been her eighteenth birthday. She had wept bitterly throughout the whole day for the loss of Burke Sinclair, her first love and the man she longed to marry. They had promised themselves to each other, had sworn to find a way to keep their love alive, but her father, Murray Sutherland, had forbidden them from ever seeing each other. He even threatened all-out war with the Sinclairs if Burke ever came near her again.

Her father had arranged for what he considered a more suitable match for Meredith—Chisolm Sutherland, a distant cousin on her mother's side and a fellow clansman. Her father didn't seem to mind that Chisolm was older than her by nearly two score. It was best for the clan, he had said to her sternly on her wedding day.

After all, Meredith and her brother Ansel were the immediate cousins to the only legitimate male heir in line for the Sutherland Lairdship. That meant that if anything happened to Kenneth Sutherland, the only son of the current Laird, Ansel would be next in line to take over. Meredith had to do her duty by shoring up clan ties and strengthening the connections between their family and the rest of the clan, her father had explained.

After her father had thoroughly chastised her for her selfishness and girlish sorrow, Meredith was quickly cinched into a fine gown, her tears scrubbed away by a hurried hand. Then she was pushed down the stairs of Brora Tower to be presented to her groom.

Chisolm had been annoyed with Meredith even before he saw her for the first time. He stood in the main hall of the tower house, pacing in front of the great hearth, his mostly gray hair combed back from his wrinkled features. When he noticed her approaching from the stairwell, his cold eyes had slid over her, half in appraisal of his young bride, and half in disdain for her red-rimmed eyes and trembling lower lip.

The ceremony was over practically before it began. After a few quick words in front of the priest, her body belonged to Chisolm. He was eager to use it, too. They'd only sat through the first half-hour of the muted celebration of their nuptials before Chisolm pulled her up to her chamber on the top floor and led her to the bed.

Without a word, he'd pushed up her skirts and lifted his kilt. Her appearance must have pleased him, she thought now with the clarity of time, for he was harder and larger than he would ever be again in the coming years. He had tried to push into her, but the dry friction and her own innocence prevented it. She'd bit her tongue on a cry of pain, trying to remain motionless so that the moment would be over quicker.

She remembered how he had cursed under his breath. Then came the act that would begin and exemplify their marital relationship. He spat into his hand and reached between her legs, his cold fingers swiping over her sex. She jerked back uncontrollably at the contact, but his hips kept her legs open. With one hard thrust, he was inside her.

Then she could no longer suppress the cry that rose in her throat. The pain had torn through her, and she'd tried to pull away, but he held her firm, thrusting a few more times before groaning and collapsing onto her. She'd held her breath, letting the tears slide silently down into her hair and the bed's coverlet.

After a few minutes, Chisolm said something vaguely complimentary, then stood, righting his kilt. He returned to the celebration below without a backward glance.

Meredith had pulled her skirts down and curled into a ball on her bed, muffling the pained sobs with her pillow. Thus began ten years of marriage.

She inhaled the fresh summer air again, trying to chase away the dark memories. At least it had gotten somewhat more tolerable as the years stretched on. At first, Chisolm was insistent, urgent even, like that first time. He would corner her in the stairwell or roll on top of her in the middle of the night, not waiting for her body to adjust to his touch, but simply thrusting into her.

But after the first few years, when it became apparent that he could not get his heir on her, he grew more sullen and distant. She hated his silence and his cold dismissal of her, but she clung to the fact that he no longer touched her.

There was a brief stretch in their marriage when Chisolm had yelled at her, berated her, and even accused her of some sort of wrongdoing for not getting pregnant, but that passed soon enough. She was well aware that he had seduced several of their household staff, spending more energy wooing and bedding them that he ever had on her. Even still, none of the maids ever became pregnant either. No one spoke of it openly, but all of Brora Tower knew that Chisolm would not have an heir.

And now Chisolm Sutherland was dead. She had done her duty, both to her family and to her late husband. She had sat by his bedside during the illness that would eventually take his life, silently holding vigil despite the fact that he all but ignored her. His soul was in God's hands now, and she was free of him.

Her chest squeezed painfully at the thought, even as her pulse ticked up in nervous anticipation. What did it mean to be free of Chisolm? Though she had never loved him, and even hated him at times for his treatment, a life without his cold, demanding presence suddenly seemed like uncharted territory. Who was she, if not the wife of Chisolm Sutherland?

Was she simply Murray Sutherland's daughter? Her father had died not long after the wedding. Though he had never said it, his eyes carried the guilt of the ill-formed union in his last few weeks of life. Her father had probably assumed that she would quickly forget her puppy-love for Burke. Or perhaps he didn't fully grasp Chisolm's character until he was living under the same roof with the man. Either way, it was too late. The match had been made, and Meredith had been forced to live with the consequences.

Perhaps she was just Ansel Sutherland's sister. Her brother had already begun to be groomed for the Lairdship before their father had died, but the training picked up even more afterward. Not long after their father's passing, Ansel had been called to Dunrobin, the Sutherland clan castle a few dozen miles from Brora Tower for further preparations alongside Kenneth Sutherland.

She only saw him a few times a year despite Brora's proximity to Dunrobin. Ansel was busy, though. He helped the clan and its lands run smoothly by aiding first their uncle and then their cousin Kenneth in any way he could. And with the increased activity by the English army in Scotland, along with Robert the Bruce's rebellion, it seemed like Ansel was constantly traveling to either battles or negotiations.

A chirp overhead brought Meredith's head snapping up. She caught sight of a flash of brown and red as a little bird darted above her. It must be a male linnet, she thought as her eyes followed the swoops and darts of the bird. He had on his summer plumage, which was mostly brown but with red at the head and chest.

The little bird trilled again, and Meredith heard a response from somewhere off to the west. The linnet swooped easily toward the sound, and was soon lost to her sight. She couldn't help but smile at the bird's easy movement. It stirred a long-forgotten memory in her, almost like a hazy dream.

She used to love animals. She would tromp out to the woods a few miles away from Brora Tower and watch birds or squirrels for hours at a time. Once, she had slipped into her father's study and used some of his expensive parchment to sketch dozens of animals from memory. She had received a severe swatting for doing so, but it hadn't dampened her appetite to study animals.

Burke Sinclair's face suddenly swam forth from the depths of her memory. She was so startled at the unbidden image of the handsome young man from her past that she gasped out loud. What had called the image of his face from the recesses of her mind?

The fox. She smiled at the memory of herself as a girl—nay, a young woman—chasing after a beautiful red fox on a cold winter's evening. That was the night she first met Burke.

The memory was bittersweet. Over the years, she had become skilled at pushing away thoughts of Burke. At first, she had clung to the image of his face, his whispered words and soft kisses. But as time passed, she realized that although thoughts of him warmed her inside, they only made her real life seem colder, highlighting her present pain and unhappiness.

Now, though, she leaned into the memories. She let them wash over her like the sunlight that warmed her face as she stood on the roof of the tower.

Burke's sandy hair, which he kept having to push back from his face whenever he leaned toward her.

His blue eyes, which were somehow darker and deeper than the North Sea, yet which danced when he smiled.

His firm body pressed against hers.

A slight breeze from the east caressed her heated skin and ruffled her hair and dress. Even the simple act of allowing herself to remember made her feel more alive than she had in years. Perhaps this was who she truly was—not a wife or a daughter or a sister, but a woman, feeling the sunshine on her hair and the wind on her skin, watching the birds flit through the perfect summer sky and thinking of love.

It was a start, anyway. Chisolm Sutherland was dead. And Meredith Sutherland was coming back to life.

Chapter Three

By the time Burke finally dismounted and unrolled an extra length of plaid to sleep on, the summer sun had set and the bluish light of night was setting in.

He was in Sutherland territory now. Both he and Laoch were exhausted, but deep sleep evaded him. Though the night was warm and the forest floor soft, he couldn't get comfortable. Bloody hell, but Sutherland land was no place for a lone Sinclair, he thought for the hundredth time.

The following morning a few hours into his ride, he halted Laoch near a large loch. He let the animal drink, then hobbled him and knelt next to the water's edge, cupping his hands in the cool, clear water. When he had taken his fill, he stood, scanning the area.

Sutherland land looked similar to Sinclair land, though the Sinclair coastline, on the very farthest northeast tip of Scotland, was a bit more rugged. Burke was surrounded by patches of forest, which were broken up by rolling green hills and taller mountains to the west. He couldn't quite see the coast to the east, but he knew that if he were atop one of the nearby hills, he would be able to spot the North Sea. The loch at which he stood was longer than it was wide, and he could look up the length of it as it continued northwesterly.

Suddenly a sense of familiarity slammed into him. It was unlikely that he had been here before, though. Since tensions remained high between the Sutherlands and the Sinclairs, he and his clansmen normally took the long way around Sutherland land. The only time he could remember traveling directly across Sutherland terrain, as he did now, was...

That night in November, nearly ten years ago. It felt like a lifetime ago. The summer scene transformed before his eyes into the wintery landscape of that cold, stormy night...

November, 1297

Burke tried to suppress the shiver that threatened to make him look like a green lad in front of his uncle, three cousins, and the handful of other clansmen who were traveling south. Despite his thick woolen hose, winter boots, and extra Sinclair plaid around his shoulders, there was no denying that he was freezing.

He glanced at his uncle, Laird Henry Sinclair, and noticed that his nose was tipped blue and his teeth were firmly clenched. So, even the mighty Laird was feeling the cold. Burke's cousins, Robert, Garrick, and Daniel, looked to be struggling with the unusually frigid conditions, too. Nevertheless, all the men sat stoutly atop their horses as they rode south toward the Scottish Lowlands.

They had good reason to march proudly south, this freakish winter storm be damned. They were going to witness William Wallace's knighting ceremony and pledge their clan's loyalty to the struggle for Scottish independence. Every able-bodied clansman longed to be on this trip, and Burke was honored and humbled to be part of the small retinue that was making the journey.

Burke was the cousin to the heirs of the Sinclair Lairdship, but because he was a rare only child, and a son at that, he had been sent to live and train with the Laird's three sons. He couldn't have counted himself luckier. Not only was it an honor to get to live so closely with the Laird and his family, but it made for a damned fun boyhood. He was of an age with the Sinclair brothers, and they had grown up hunting, fishing, fighting, and eventually chasing the lasses around Roslin.

Now, though, he and his Sinclair cousins were *men*. He was nineteen, which put him right between Daniel and Garrick in age. All four of them were tall, strapping, and getting bigger and stronger by the day. It seemed like none of them could get enough when it came to training with the sword, the bow, hand-to-hand combat, or learning the responsibilities of leadership.

Robert was the most serious, of course, since he would assuredly be Laird someday. Garrick excelled with the bow, and what Daniel, being the youngest, had lacked initially in age and size, he now made up for in stubborn determination and decisiveness. All agreed that Burke was the smoothest and best at talking with the lasses, but if they teased him too much about it, he was sure to give them a few scrapes and bruises on the practice field to remind them that he could fight as well.

Though relations with the Sutherlands were strained, the Sinclair retinue had been given permission to cross their lands on the way to pledge their loyalty to Wallace. The Sutherlands were on the side of Scottish independence, after all. Even still, the small band of Sinclairs moved at a brisk pace over the snow-covered hills, and it wasn't just because of the cold.

Suddenly all the men's heads snapped up at the faint sound of a high-pitched scream.

"What the devil?" Laird Sinclair said gruffly, wheeling his horse toward the sound.

"Nay, father, it could be dangerous," Robert said at the Laird's side.

"We cannot let fear prevent us from doing what is right," the Laird replied quietly to his eldest son. He motioned for the group of men to follow him and spurred his horse in the direction of the sound.

Burke's blood was suddenly warmer, and it wasn't from the increased pace of the warhorse beneath him.

What could have made such a sound? Would he and his clansmen be able to help?

The band of Sinclair men didn't have to travel far through the deep snowdrifts and biting wind to discover the source of the scream. A frozen loch emerged ahead through the flurries of snow. While most of the surface was frozen over and still, Burke's eye immediately went to the flutter of movement along the nearest shoreline.

The scream came again, and this time there was no mistaking it—it came from a thrashing figure who had apparently fallen through the ice. It sounded like a lass.

Without thinking, Burke kicked his horse hard, sending him shooting ahead of the others. His eyes were locked on the figure, who was flailing and keening with increasing desperation. He vaguely registered his uncle's calls for caution behind him, but he ignored them.

He reined in his horse just at the loch's frozen shoreline and flung himself from the animal's back. Never taking his eyes from the thrashing figure, he ripped off the extra plaids he had wrapped around his shoulders, then stepped cautiously onto the ice.

Just as he eased onto the iced-over loch, the rest of the party arrived at the shoreline. Burke didn't wait for them, though. Instead, he moved toward the helpless lass, ignoring the sting of cold cutting through his clothes. Again, shouts sounded from behind him, but he was entirely focused on the flailing figure, who was now only a few yards away.

She was struggling to keep her head above the icy water. Her screams had turned to strangled gurgles. As Burke neared her, he crouched, then slid his belly onto the ice to avoid breaking through himself. The pool in which the lass swam was large, indicating that she had tried to pull herself out, only to break off more of the icy crust.

"It's all right, lass," Burke said in a low, soothing tone as he inched himself forward on his stomach.

Her wide, dark eyes locked on him with a look of terror and desperation, and he felt a jolt in his chest.

"Just swim over here and I'll pull you out." He spoke as if he were trying to sooth a spooked animal.

She struggled feebly toward him. No doubt her limbs were turning to stone from the cold. He had to act fast if he hoped to save her. He extended his arm, shortening the distance and coaxing her on with a beckoning hand.

Her head slipped a bit lower in the water even as she strained to reach his outstretched hand. He scooted an inch closer, but froze when he heard the deep groan of the ice beneath him.

"Just a little farther, lass. That's it. You can do it. Reach!"

Just as her head sank completely under the dark water, her fingers brushed his. He risked lurching forward even farther. Blessedly, instead of falling through the ice himself, he managed to clamp a hand around her wrist and yank her toward him.

She slid like a seal onto the ice next to him, coughing and sputtering violently. He scooted himself farther back onto more solid ice, dragging her by the wrist after him. When he felt it was safe, he raised himself first to a crouch, then onto one knee, all the while listening to the ice. The only noise, though, was the lass's haggard breathing and the distant sounds of his clansmen on the shore, who were calling out encouragements to him.

When he fully trusted the ice, he knelt and scooped the shivering, coughing lass in his arms. Despite the fact that he had been lying on the ice with only his shirt to protect him from the cold, his skin felt warm in comparison to her drenched, huddled body. She wasn't out of the woods yet.

As quickly as he could manage without slipping, Burke strode to the loch's shore. Several of his clansmen ripped the extra plaids from their own shoulders and wrapped them around both him and the lass.

"What the bloody hell brought about that course of action, Burke?" Laird Sinclair said as he vigorously rubbed Burke's back through several layers of plaid.

"I…I just…I knew I needed to help her," he replied, though judging by the Laird's furrowed brow, the explanation made about as much sense to him as it did to Burke himself. He didn't know what had possessed him to act so rashly. All he knew was that something in the lass's cries had stabbed him directly in the heart, and he had to save her.

He looked down at the slight lass in his arms. Her long, dark hair was plastered to her head, and her wide eyes were still locked on him with a look somewhere between awe and disbelief. For some reason, his chest pulled again, and his stomach did a little flip.

Just then, he registered her sodden wool cloak and gown. The weight of those garments had nearly drowned her, and now they were holding the cold water to her skin.

The Laird seemed to have the same thought. "She needs to get warm. Dougall, where is the nearest Sutherland keep?"

The gnarled old clansman thought for a moment. "Brora Tower isn't far from here, Laird. We skirted it a few miles back," Dougall said finally.

The lass nodded vigorously. "B-B-Brora," she managed through chattering teeth.

"Lass, you'll also need to…discard those soaked clothes," Laird Sinclair said, averting his eyes.

The lass's eyes widened even more, and her gaze shot from Burke to the Laird and the surrounding men.

"Don't misunderstand," the Laird said quickly, holding up his hands. "We are not interested in compromising the honor of a Sutherland lass. But you could die if you don't get warmed up, and fast. We can keep you covered with our plaids the whole time, and we'll all turn our backs while you disrobe."

After another futile glance at the group of men, she

nodded again. She reached for the tie holding her cloak closed at her neck, and though her fingers shook violently, she managed to unfasten the tie. With a few adjustments of his arms, which still firmly held the lass to his chest, Burke managed to free the sodden cloak, and the garment dropped heavily into the snow at his feet. Laird Sinclair scooped it up and draped it across his saddle.

Burke set the lass down so that she could begin working on her dress, and all the Sinclair men moved off several paces with their backs turned. But when the lass's feet touched the ground and her weight came onto them, she cried out and nearly toppled over. Burke instantly wrapped her in his embrace once more, steadying her.

"M-m-my legs d-d-don't seem to b-b-be working," she stuttered through her shivers.

Desperate to help but unsure of what to do, Burke glanced around. His eyes lighted on a copse of evergreen trees a few dozen yards away. "Perhaps I can help," he said, scooping her off her feet again.

He strode to the copse and set the lass down again, but this time, he placed her on a fallen log so that she didn't have to use her frozen legs or feet. She began fumbling with the ties on her dress, but her fingers couldn't manage the small knots.

After watching her struggle for several moments, Burke tentatively reached out and glanced at her for permission to help. She nodded silently, so he set to work on the gown's ties. In short order, he had the ties loosened, but hesitated again at what to do next.

"It's all right," the lass said, apparently reading the uncertainty on his face. She reached up to the material at her shoulders and feebly pulled it down, but the soaked wool barely budged. So Burke helped her again, tugging down her dress even as he felt his face flame.

Despite his cousins' teasing about his skill with the lasses, the encounters he'd had—a few stolen kisses with a kitchen maid, a bit more with a lass from the village last Beltane—all seemed tame and boyish compared to this. He had saved this beautiful, ethereal lass, and now he was helping her disrobe.

He ripped both his thoughts and his eyes away from what his hands were doing as they tugged her dress past her breasts and down her waist to reveal her soaked chemise. He was only doing this out of necessity, he reminded himself. He forced his eyes to stay firmly focused over her right shoulder, but even still, his hands brushed the inward curve of her waist and the flare of her hips, and he felt a stab of heat despite the frosty temperature.

She scooted a bit so that he could pull the dress across her seated bottom and down her slim legs. He nearly sighed with—was it relief or disappointment?—when the task was complete. But then he made the mistake of bringing his eyes back to her, and he inhaled sharply.

The wet chemise left almost nothing to his imagination. He could see the delicate curve of her breasts where the material plastered to her skin. Each one was tipped with a rosy, hard bead, which stood out clearly.

He jerked and spun on his heels, giving her his back. "Do you think you can…ahem…manage to remove your chemise on your own?"

"Aye," she said in a strained voice behind him. Had he embarrassed her with his hands and roaming eyes? He felt like a lout, but his blood fired hotter than ever.

"And thank you," she said after a brief pause. Did he mistake a note of breathiness in her voice?

He heard rustling as she removed her chemise, and if he had felt hot before, now he was incinerated. The lass was naked behind him. He tried to rein in his thoughts, but failed when she tugged one of the Sinclair plaids from his shoulders. She would be wrapped in nothing but his plaid. That was by far more intimate than anything he had experienced.

He kept his back to her until she spoke. "All right. You can turn around now."

Her dark, damp hair spilled all around the red of the Sinclair plaid, which was wound tight around her shoulders. Her snow-white skin stood in stark contrast to the plaid and her hair. Burke nearly gasped at her beauty.

Luckily, the plaid was both long and wide. It covered her past the knees. She still wore boots, and despite the fact that they too were soaking wet, Burke thought it best to avoid direct contact with the snow underfoot.

He took up her discarded dress and chemise, then removed another one of the extra plaids his clansmen had placed on his shoulders and draped it around her. When she was snugly wrapped up, he scooped her up from the fallen log and strode back to the others. Some of the men had already mounted in preparation to ride back toward Brora Tower.

When Burke reached his horse, he set the lass down long enough to quickly snatch up the plaids he had initially tossed from his shoulders. He offered them to his clansmen, who had given him their own plaids, but none would take them, insisting that he give them to the lass instead. She watched him silently as she leaned against his horse for balance, her eyes penetrating him.

Laird Sinclair approached, forcing Burke to tear his thoughts from the lass. The Laird took the dress and chemise from Burke and draped them over his saddle with the cloak, then turned to her.

"What is your name, lass?"

"Meredith. Meredith Sutherland."

"And you live at Brora Tower?"

"Aye. My father will be most grateful to you for saving me." Her eyes flitted to Burke, then back to the Laird.

"And who is your father?"

"Murray Sutherland."

The Laird rubbed his beard. "Laird Sutherland's

brother?"

"Aye."

Laird Sinclair's face darkened slightly. Though he was still young and not privy to all the goings-on behind the Laird's solar door, Burke knew that Laird Sinclair had a particularly black opinion of both Laird Sutherland and his brother Murray. Those two men seemed determined to keep relations sour and tense between the Sutherlands and the Sinclairs. It was a miracle that the Sinclairs had even been granted permission to travel through Sutherland land. Likely, the Sutherlands hoped the Sinclair retinue would succumb to the frigid conditions and never make it to their destination.

Schooling his features, the Laird gave the lass an encouraging nod, then turned to Burke. "Keep her warm, lad. We still have several miles to go before we make it back to Brora Tower."

Burke nodded solemnly, but his stomach did a little flip again. He would have to share his body heat with her, rub her to get the circulation going again…. Burke certainly wasn't having any problems with circulation at the moment—at least in one particular area.

He mounted his horse, and with the help of Robert and the Laird, he hoisted the lass up onto his lap. She still shivered, and he reminded himself that this was no time to let his mind—or any other body part—get distracted.

He adjusted the plaid he had wrapped around his

own shoulders so that it encased both of them. Then he took the reins in one hand, keeping the other firmly tucked around her. She leaned into him, trying to soak up some of his warmth, so he rubbed her arm and back vigorously as the party turned to the northeast and headed toward Brora Tower.

Despite the icy wind and the flurries of snow, Burke's blood ran hot in his veins. He and this Sutherland lass were creating a little cocoon of heat between them. As the warmth started to seep back into her limbs, she sighed and grew increasingly limp in his arms.

He prayed she couldn't feel his swelling length under her bottom. He had to find a way to distract himself.

"What made you decide to take a bath in the loch on such a fine and balmy evening, Meredith Sutherland?" he said as lightly as he could manage.

She tilted her head up so that she could meet his gaze. At first, her dark brown eyes were wide with surprise, but when she picked up on his teasing tone, she smiled faintly, and a pretty blush pinkened her pale skin.

"I was chasing a fox."

He raised his eyebrows at her. "A fox? What could a fox do to compel you to cross thin ice? Did he steal a kiss from you?"

This drew a giggle from the lass, and he noticed the faint smattering of freckles across the bridge of her nose as it wrinkled in merriment.

Bloody hell. So much for distracting himself. He had only meant to lighten the mood and jest a bit with the lass, but now he was talking about stolen kisses.

"Nay, nothing so dastardly as that!" she said, snuggling into him. "I just thought he was…beautiful." The last word was spoken guardedly, as if she expected him to laugh at her, or chastise her.

Instead, he grew serious. "A fox is indeed a beautiful sight, lass. Was it your first time spotting one?"

"Nay, but I've never seen one so close before. He had a white tip on his tail. Have you seen such a thing before?"

Burke considered. "Nay, I can't say that I have." Then he went on gently. "So you chased after him and fell through the ice?"

"Aye, I wasn't paying attention. He kept going a little farther, and then so would I, and then…" She shook her head a little, likely to chase away the terrifying events. But then she turned her dark stare on him again. "I am very…moved by animals. I love to watch them, draw them—anything. They seem so much more…*pure* than people."

There was a note of pleading in her voice, like she wanted to be understood. But Burke wasn't sure what to say, so he simply squeezed her a little tighter with his arm. That seemed to communicate more to her than words could have, for she nestled her head under his chin.

"What is the name of the man who saved my life?" she said into his chest.

"Burke Sinclair," he said, feeling a swell of pride.

"Burke Sinclair. I'll not forget you," she said softly.

All too soon, Dougall pointed up ahead to a stone structure rising from the top of a snow-covered hill. The tower house was several stories tall like a tower inside a castle, but unlike a castle, no curtain wall surrounded it. A barn and a few other outbuildings stood nearby, but the house itself was mostly isolated.

If Burke's sense of direction was right, they were several miles inland and to the northwest of Dunrobin, the Sutherland clan seat. This tower house could have been used as a lookout for Dunrobin Castle. If someone lit a fire on the rooftop of the tower, the flames and smoke could be seen from miles away, warning Dunrobin of an attack.

Plus, though it was not as fortified as a castle, the tower house could withstand a small attack. From Burke's view on his saddle, the stone walls rose imposingly, and a large family and their household staff could likely hole up there for weeks at a time.

Burke and the others reined in their horses when they reached the base of the tower.

"Hello, Brora Tower! We come in peace!" Laird Sinclair said in a loud, clear voice.

The furs covering one of the narrow windows on the top floor rustled and a head appeared.

"What is your business here?" a voice called down.

"We have Meredith Sutherland with us. She fell through some ice, but my nephew rescued her."

The head disappeared and the furs settled back over the window. The men waited, and after a long stretch, the heavy door at the base of the tower creaked open. There stood an imposing, barrel-chested man with a dark beard and a Sutherland plaid wrapped around his shoulders.

"I am Murray Sutherland, the lass's father. Give her to me," he said, eyeing them suspiciously.

Burke dismounted and reached for Meredith, bringing her down to his side. Murray Sutherland's eyes widened as he took in the sight of his daughter, her hair damp and bedraggled, her body clothed only in a Sinclair plaid. He stepped forward and took her by the arm, jerking her behind him as if to shield her from the very men who'd rescued her.

"Get inside, Meredith," he said in a clipped tone over his shoulder. She hurried through the tower door as fast as her stiff legs could take her.

"Perhaps we might warm ourselves at your hearth for a few moments, Sutherland," Laird Sinclair said carefully.

Murray spat into the snow, but after a moment, he reluctantly nodded. The men dismounted and slowly filed into the tower. Several of them exchanged looks, unsure whether they were grateful for the warmth of a fire or uneasy at accepting a Sutherland's grudging hospitality.

They wouldn't turn down a fire in these conditions, though. Warm air blasted Burke as he entered the Tower's main floor, which was an open hall used for dining and entertaining. In the far wall, a fire roared in an enormous hearth, and Burke followed the others like moths to the flame.

Laird Sinclair introduced himself and his men, though Murray seemed to already know a few of them. Likely, they had met at some tense Highland clan caucus to try to keep relations functioning. Or worse, Burke suddenly realized, perhaps they had encountered each other in some skirmish or raid.

The Laird handed Sutherland Meredith's soggy cloak and dress, then explained how they had found the lass, and how Burke had saved her from an almost certain death. Sutherland grunted and shifted his gaze to Burke, assessing him.

"My thanks, lad," he said simply, though it looked like it pained him.

Just then, Meredith emerged from the stairwell in the back corner of the hall. She had donned a dry wool dress of dark blue, and her hair looked substantially drier, but she still wore Burke's Sinclair plaid around her shoulders. Her eyes immediately sought him, and a faint smile and tinge of pink touched her face.

"Father, these men saved my life," she said as she approached, though she never took her eyes from Burke.

"Aye, so they have said," Sutherland replied sourly.

"I thank you again. Now I think it is time for you to leave."

Laird Sinclair's face turned stony, but he nodded. "Aye. Thank you for your hospitality," he said curtly.

Just as Burke turned reluctantly to go, he felt a small hand on his forearm. He turned to find Meredith's beautiful, dark eyes holding him. "Thank you. I'll never forget you," she said in a near-whisper that felt private and intimate.

Just then, Murray snatched the Sinclair plaid from around her shoulders and tossed it toward Burke.

"She'll not be needing that anymore," he said coldly.

Burke caught the plaid and exchanged a hard look with Sutherland, but before his hotheaded youth could take over, his Laird called him from the door of the tower.

"It's best we keep moving, Burke," the Laird said pointedly.

With one last glance at Meredith's upturned face, which was now clouded with hurt and confusion at her father's brusqueness, Burke turned and exited the tower. Without ado, the tower door was closed firmly behind him. He mounted his horse along with the others and headed back through their own tracks in the snow.

He couldn't resist one last look, though. Glancing over his shoulder, he caught sight of a dark head peeking behind the furs of a high window. Even from the ever-stretching distance between them, he could feel Meredith's eyes on him. He shivered despite the heat that coursed through his veins.

Chapter Four

Late November, 1297

Two weeks after Meredith's eyes had first seared into him, Burke rode toward Brora Tower, but alone this time. His pulse hitched in anticipation. He had vowed never to forget those dark, depthless eyes and the way they seemed to penetrate him to his soul. And soon he would be held in Meredith's deep gaze once more.

He and his clansmen had ridden to the Borderlands with a sour taste in their mouths at Murray Sutherland's rude treatment. Still, it had been an honor to see William Wallace knighted, and to be part of the retinue that would pledge the Sinclair clan's loyalty to Wallace and the rebellion.

Of course, Burke had barely registered the events of their trip after that snowy evening with Meredith Sutherland. It was like he was sleepwalking, and he couldn't shake the dream of Meredith's eyes or her rosy lips, the slim curves that had been pressed against him under his plaid, or her innocent but passionate words about her love of animals.

To earn this side trip to see her again, he had begged his uncle on their return through Sutherland lands to let him peel off from the others and pay a visit to Brora Tower. At first, Laird Sinclair had outright refused Burke's pleas, but it was obvious to all the men that Burke was determined. Eventually, he managed to wear the Laird down, and Burke was granted a few hours' detour as they passed nearby.

As Burke neared the base of the tower, he jumped eagerly from his horse's back even before the animal had come to a complete halt.

But when he knocked on the tower's door and asked permission to speak with Meredith, he was told in no uncertain terms by Murray Sutherland that he could not see her and that he had better make haste off Sutherland lands.

The tower door slammed with a thud in his face. Desperate and frustrated, Burke circled around to the other side of the tower and gazed up at the high windows. Meredith was so close, yet the unforgiving stone walls of the tower separated them.

Just then, the furs covering one of the windows rustled and there she was. Her chestnut hair spilled in wild waves out the window, and when she spotted him below, a smile lit up her face.

"I thought I heard my father sending you away!" she said in her loudest whisper.

"Aye, but I won't give up. I must see you, Meredith."

She giggled a little, though she tried to cover it with her hand. "And I must see you, Burke Sinclair. Wait here. I have an idea."

Before he could respond, her head vanished back through the window. But a moment later, a rope ladder unfurled almost to the ground. She reappeared, and turning sideways through the window, she eased one foot and then the other onto the ladder. The windows were too narrow for a full-grown man—especially one wearing armor, as the English did—to pass through, but Meredith had no trouble slipping out.

When she was on the bottom rung, she turned and spontaneously launched herself the remaining few feet toward the ground. But instead of landing in the snow, which still lingered after the intense storm two weeks earlier, she ended up in Burke's waiting arms.

Slowly, reluctantly, he eased her down the length of his body until her feet touched the ground. Her breath caught in her throat and her eyes sought his in a lingering look.

Suddenly glancing around nervously, she took his hand and pulled him toward one of the outbuildings nearby. When she slid open the wooden door, Burke realized it was the barn. The smell of warm animals and fresh hay hit him as she guided him inside and closed the door.

"I like to come here to be alone," she said over her shoulder as she led him to the back of the barn. "But I don't mind sharing my thinking place with you."

He followed her as she climbed the ladder into the hay loft at the far end of the barn. As he sat next to her in the hay, he noticed that the wooden boards at the back of the loft were—not marred, he realized as he looked closer, but carved. He made out the shapes of deer, hawks, rabbits, and even foxes and wolves. She had carved the animal figures here in secret, and she was sharing that secret with him.

Her eyes followed his, and her cheeks flamed in embarrassment. "Those are just—"

Before she could say more, he leaned in and brushed his lips against hers.

He had thought of doing nothing else ever since he had first laid eyes on her, yet it was sweeter and more enticing than anything his mind could conjure. Her soft, dark pink lips yielded to him like warm honey. He caught a whiff of roses coming from her chestnut tresses. When he pulled back, her cheeks were pink and her lips were softly parted in surprise, yet her dark eyes told him she felt the same desire he did.

They spend the entire afternoon talking, kissing, and lying next to each other in the hay up in the loft. Time stretched, and Burke knew he had long overstayed his Laird's allowance of two hours.

Eventually, Meredith admitted that she would be needed in the tower soon. If they noticed that she wasn't in her room and that the ladder was down, their little secret would be spoiled forever.

Burke promised to return as soon as he could manage to get away from Roslin. As they shared one last goodbye kiss, tears shimmered in Meredith's eyes. She turned away before any of them slipped down her smooth cheeks.

Burke walked her back to the ladder and helped her get onto the first rung. He watched as she climbed up and slipped through her window, then pulled the ladder back inside. Even after she waved one last time to him and let the furs settle back over the window, he stood staring up at where she had been, longing to see more of her.

After another moment, though, the thought of his waiting Laird worried him enough to send him hurrying to his horse and back to his clansmen a few miles away.

By the time he got back to them, the sun had set and the sky was dark. Laird Sinclair bent Burke's ear long and hard with admonitions for his thoughtless, reckless behavior. All the while, though, Burke couldn't suppress a wide grin. This seemed to only anger the Laird further, though it brought no end of amusement to his three cousins, who teased him mercilessly on their ride back to Roslin.

Burke didn't care. He was madly, hopelessly, undeniably in love.

Burke managed to steal away from Roslin and meet secretly with Meredith three more times over the course of that winter. Each time, they kissed, embraced, and explored each other, both with their hands and through conversations that would stretch for hours.

When the first hints of spring breathed new life into the land, Burke finally got up the nerve to ask Murray Sutherland for permission to marry his daughter.

He was refused.

He asked again.

Again, he was refused, less politely than the first time. The tower's door slammed in his face, muffling Sutherland's curses and threats to geld him if he came near his daughter again.

The third time he pounded on Brora Tower's door would be the last.

Burke again reasoned with Sutherland, begged him, tried to bargain with him. He told Sutherland that although he was only nineteen, he would provide for Meredith. Burke reminded him that he had saved Meredith's life, that a wedding between the clans might do everyone good, that he was in love with her and would never do wrong by her.

This time, instead of yelling at him or cursing him, Sutherland stood silently in the doorway. When Burke had exhausted himself with reasons why he should be allowed to marry Meredith, Sutherland spoke.

"Meredith is to be married to another tomorrow," he said simply.

Sutherland might as well have run Burke through with the large sword strapped to his hip.

"What?"

"All the arrangements have already been made. I would never let her be wed to some…*Sinclair*. She will wed a clansman, someone who will improve the clan and the family."

Burke stood there, his jaw slack and his eyes wide, refusing to believe what he was hearing.

"Now, I suggest you leave here and never return," Sutherland went on coldly.

When Burke continued to stand motionless and open-mouthed, a crack finally appeared in Sutherland's stony exterior.

"If you really care for her as much as you claim, then you will leave her alone and forget about her. You can only make things harder on her by lingering here, or worse, interfering with her marriage."

Burke thought he heard muffled sobs coming from higher up in the tower. He glanced up, but all he saw were the cold, uncaring stones of the tower's walls.

Burke was a man of honor. He had to put his own feelings, and Meredith's, aside if she was to be another's wife. Perhaps one day they could each be happy, even though they would never be together. His insides twisted at the thought, rejecting it, but what else could he do besides ride back to Sinclair lands and let Meredith go? Would he wage a war against Murray Sutherland? Would he attack Brora Tower and try to rescue Meredith again?

Nay. He would not put his entire clan and hers in jeopardy. Nor would he steal her away—even if he could—and make her an outcast from her own family.

As he turned to his horse without a word, it felt as though a piece of his heart had fallen from his chest and lay bleeding at the base of Brora Tower. Meredith Sutherland was not his to love, and she never would be.

Chapter Five

July, 1307

Laoch strode smoothly beneath him, though Burke barely remembered leaving the loch and heading out once again, so lost in thought was he.

Ahead of him, he spotted a tower rising from a green, rolling hill. His heart sank. Without realizing it, he had guided Laoch toward Brora Tower.

He was about to pull the stallion sharply northward, but he paused. Nearly ten years had passed since he had last seen Meredith or the tower. Curiosity niggled at him. What harm would it do just to look—from a safe distance, of course—at the tower?

He spurred Laoch on, halting just at the edge of a copse of trees so that he would remain relatively obscured from view.

The sight of the tower still stirred him. He gazed at it for several long moments, especially the window through which Meredith used to appear whenever they would have one of their secret rendezvous.

Just then, a flicker of movement along the landing

surrounding the tower's roof caught his eye. He glanced up, and his stomach tumbled to the ground like a boulder.

Could it be her?

A woman leaned against the tower's parapet, her chestnut hair blowing gently in the summer breeze. She was thin, frail almost, but the quiet, graceful set of her shoulders was unmistakable.

Meredith.

She had lost all traces of her girlish playfulness, which were replaced with a somber yet ethereal grace. Her skin was paler than he remembered, but he could make out her dark eyes even from this distance.

She turned her head a little toward him, as if she sensed his presence. He thought of guiding Laoch further back into the copse, but a movement would only draw her attention more, so he sat motionless, gazing up at her. Even though he remained still, her eyes locked on him, and he could see that her lips parted in a surprised gasp.

Without thinking, he dug his heels into Laoch's sides, sending him bolting from the copse of trees and past the tower toward the northeast.

He spurred Laoch into a gallop, trying to run away from the tower and the beautiful apparition of Meredith Sutherland as fast as he could.

He was a coward—a coward and a fool for thinking that he could innocently see Brora Tower or Meredith ever again. He had made his choice ten years ago—or rather, Murray Sutherland had made their choices for them. Why would he still hold out hope all these years later that the pain of the past could be erased?

Chapter Six

Burke rode hard through the raised portcullis in the curtain wall of Roslin Castle. He tossed the reins to a stable lad and slid from Laoch's back just as Robert, Laird of the Sinclair clan, arrived in the courtyard.

"Where is Garrick?" Robert said, his voice laced with concern for his younger brother, who was supposed to return with Burke.

"All is well, Robert. He went to the Bruce's camp with the same news that I must share with you."

Robert's already stormy countenance darkened. Just then, though, Lady Alwin, Robert's wife, waddled from the keep into the yard behind him. Even in the month or so since he had seen her, she had grown much bigger with the heir to the Sinclair Lairdship.

"Burke!" she huffed, a strained smile on her face. "You've returned! I'll have a meal prepared and send a bath to your room."

Robert turned to his pregnant wife and spoke in a low voice, though Burke could hear him. "Alwin, what have I told you about overextending yourself? You should be resting in the solar."

Alwin waved him away as if he were a fly, but her eyes held warmth and merriment for her husband and his concern. "Nonsense. I am perfectly able to see to Burke's comfort after what looks to have been a long and harrowing journey."

Her eyes appraised him, and Burke realized that he must look terrible. His clothes were soiled with dirt and blood. His hair was pulled back and fastened at his neck, but he hadn't shaved in at least a few weeks, and the light brown scruff could rightly be called a beard now.

"Thank you, Lady Alwin. I will be grateful for a hot meal and a bath, but I must speak with the Laird first. It is pressing," he said, shifting his eyes to Robert.

Robert nodded curtly. He motioned for Burke to follow him into the keep and toward a small meeting room off the main hall. Alwin peeled off from them once they were inside, calling out orders for food and a bath to the kitchen staff.

Once the heavy wooden door of the small, dim meeting room was shut, Burke launched into an account of the events of the last few weeks. Robert listened silently as he leaned back in a sturdy chair, his hand occasionally coming up to rub his chin in thought.

Burke told of Garrick and his successful information gathering in Dunbraes Village, and their encounter with a healer lass named Jossalyn. When

Burke described how Jossalyn had stowed away with them on their way back north into Scotland, Robert frowned but remained silent.

But then the heart of Burke's news had the Laird sitting bolt upright, a dark scowl on his face and a cold fire in his pale blue eyes. Burke repeated the words that had shaken him to his core that day several weeks ago on the outskirts of Dunbraes: Longshanks was dead.

The Hammer of the Scots could no longer torment them, but his son, Edward II, could prove to be even worse than his father. Only time would tell, but regardless, King Edward I was dead.

Robert remained rigid and perched on the edge of his seat as Burke described Raef Warren's return to Dunbraes, Garrick's rescue of Jossalyn, who was actually Warren's sister, the battle that ensued, and their flight north. They were somewhat delayed because of the wound Burke had received to his leg, but Jossalyn had tended to it, and had probably saved Burke's life.

Robert ran a hand through his hair, his eyes shifting across the ceiling in thought. "Longshanks is dead. And Warren still eludes us." He sprang from his chair and began pacing the small room.

"We were lucky to escape with our lives. But Warren's time will come, I'm sure of it."

"And Garrick opted to return to the Bruce's camp to deliver this news?" Robert's voice tightened with annoyance at his younger brother's disregard for the direct order to return to Roslin.

"Aye, with Lady Jossalyn," Burke replied.

That had Robert's brows shooting up in surprise. Burke tried to keep his features blank. Garrick could deliver the news of his love for Lady Jossalyn—if the stubborn fool could ever admit it to himself.

Even though he schooled his features to perfect smoothness, Robert knew Burke too well.

"My brother and Raef Warren's sister, eh?" He paced for another moment, then seemed to decide something. "I suppose that's no more preposterous than the Laird of the Sinclair clan marrying the English fiancée of that warmongering bastard."

A little smile tugged at the corners of Burke's mouth. The Sinclair men had a strange way of choosing mates, no doubt about it. But then again, Robert and Garrick were two of the luckiest, happiest men Burke had ever met when it came to their partners.

For a fleeting moment, Burke considered his place among his cousins. Like Robert and Garrick, he had chosen to fall in love with a woman who by all measures should never be his. But unlike his two older cousins, Burke reminded himself grimly, he hadn't overcome the odds and secured an unusual but joyous union.

Robert was watching him closely, so he tried to push the dark thoughts away.

"You must have made good time, even with the delays from that injury to your leg," Robert said carefully. "Which route did you take?"

"We cut east, then north to avoid Warren's search. After Garrick and Jossalyn turned east outside of Inverness, I came straight—" Suddenly it dawned on Burke what Robert was getting at. "Straight across Sutherland lands." Robert knew him too well. He should have known that his Laird and friend would guess at the cause of his suddenly dark mood.

Robert took to his chair once again and motioned for Burke to sit as well. "I've had some news myself, Burke. I heard at a recent Highland clans meeting that Chisolm Sutherland has finally passed on."

Burke was halfway seated in the chair across from Robert as the words were spoken. He collapsed the rest of the way into the chair, his legs suddenly no longer working properly.

"What?"

"Laird Kenneth Sutherland mentioned it in passing. It seems that Kenneth's cousin, Ansel, will have to leave Dunrobin soon to return to Brora Tower now that Chisolm is dead. Laird Sutherland feels the loss keenly, though I don't think he ever liked Chisolm. He's more upset to lose Ansel, who trained alongside Kenneth in the duties of Lairdship when they were lads—much like you." Robert spoke casually, as if he was simply repeating some light gossip about their neighboring clan, but Burke could feel his sharp eyes on him, watching him for his reaction.

"That means that Meredith…"

"Aye, Meredith Sutherland is a widow. She is finally free, Burke."

Burke's head spun wildly. "But the clans' feud—"

"—is so old that no one living can even remember how it started. Even old Murray Sutherland, who seemed hell-bent on keeping the feud alive, has been dead nearly ten years now."

Burke raked a hand through his hair, unable to respond. He wanted to argue, to insist that he couldn't simply return to Sutherland lands and beg once again for Meredith's hand in marriage. But Robert was right. And why would Burke try to resist the potential for happiness?

Perhaps, just as he feared when he bolted from Brora Tower after spotting Meredith on the roof, he truly was a coward. He had put that part of his life—where he had laid his heart on the line only to be refused a chance at happiness with Meredith—well behind him now. He had resigned himself to the fact that he would never have that kind of pure joy again—hadn't he?

"Burke," Robert interrupted his swirling thoughts, "I know you just got back from a long and difficult journey, but I need you to do something for me."

"Anything, Robert."

"I'd like you to meet with Ansel Sutherland to discuss the possibility of putting this ancient blood feud behind us. We both fight for the Bruce and independence from the English now. It's time we set aside our differences. Ansel Sutherland will probably already be at Brora Tower, if Laird Sutherland did indeed send him home."

Bloody hell, Robert wasn't going to make this easy. Burke would be put in Meredith's path for sure now. And she wasn't a married woman anymore. *She is free. But what if she doesn't want me anymore?* That thought sent him reeling again. Was he willing to risk his pride, his clan's honor, and even his life for the chance to have happiness with her?

Aye, he was.

It terrified him to risk himself again, to be shunned by her family for his clan of origin—or worse, to learn that she had moved on and forgotten their childish love, while for him it had remained an open wound in his life.

But he couldn't be a coward any longer. He had to face this—face her—if there was any chance for him to find happiness again.

"When shall I leave?"

"Tomorrow morning at first light."

Chapter Seven

Meredith had barely slept a wink last night.

It had been him.

It had been Burke Sinclair gazing up at her from a clump of trees near the base of the tower. No amount of time would make her forget the sandy-brown hair, strong jawline, broad shoulders, and deep blue eyes, which were visible even from the tower's roof.

And he had seen her as well. But why did he ride off without a word?

These thoughts had gnawed at her all night and through the morning, despite the many tasks and responsibilities she should be focused on as the lady of the tower. Even now, she ought to be giving her full attention to the ledgers spread open on the study's desk. Though Chisolm hadn't wanted her to become involved in clan business, he couldn't stop her from running the tower to the best of her ability now.

Just then a light knock came at the door to the study.

"Enter."

"This just came for you, milady," Beth, Meredith's

maid, said, extending a missive to her.

"Thank you, Beth."

When the maid had quietly closed the door behind her, Meredith looked down at the missive in her hand. It bore her brother's seal.

She frowned and broke the seal, hoping all was well at Dunrobin. It was unusual for Ansel to write.

But the contents of the letter were even more unusual. Ansel was returning to Brora Tower in a day, two at most. Apparently Laird Sutherland thought that since Chisolm was dead and Meredith was left to herself to oversee the tower, she needed her brother's help.

She tried to push her annoyance away. She loved her brother and should be grateful for his return, but she rankled at the idea that she couldn't run the tower as a defensive stronghold and signaler to Dunrobin without either her father, husband, or brother with her. Hadn't she done just fine when Chisolm had fallen ill last year, and also in the two weeks since his death?

No matter, she told herself firmly. Her only sibling would be back under the same roof with her once again. Without Chisolm around to prevent her from enjoying herself, perhaps she and Ansel could recapture some of the joy of their childhood.

By the time the evening meal rolled around, she was decidedly more focused and upbeat. Her brother would be back tomorrow. Burke Sinclair still lingered in her mind, but she tried to push thoughts of him aside. After all, he clearly didn't want to see or speak to her.

After the meal, she made her way up to her chamber. She slipped from her gown and unwound her braid without the help of her maid. She was suddenly tired and longed to be alone with her thoughts. Perhaps her earlier excitement for her brother's return had been more draining that she realized. Or perhaps it was the memory of dark blue eyes, soft lips, and strong, encircling arms that was making her feel weak and empty.

Just as she pulled back the coverlet on her bed, she heard a soft whistle from outside her window. She ignored it at first, dismissing it as some lark's call. As she slipped her feet under the covers, though, she realized that the sound didn't match any birdcall she knew.

The whistle came again, and her body went rigid. Could the tower be under siege? Who was lurking below, and to whom were they signaling?

She eased out of the bed and slipped silently to the window. The winter furs had been put away, but the window was still covered with shutters. As quietly and slowly as possible, she inched the shutters open a crack and peered through.

She nearly fell backward at the sight that met her eyes.

Burke Sinclair stood beneath her window!

Though he was partially shrouded in the bluish twilight, there was no mistaking his handsome face, large frame, and the dark red Sinclair plaid around his hips and over his shoulder.

"Meredith! Is that you?" he whispered up to her.

She pushed the shutters all the way open, realizing that there was no point in trying to conceal herself.

"A-aye, it's me, Burke Sinclair," she breathed shakily.

He smiled in relief, and the sun might as well have been shining directly in her face. She was struck breathless for a moment at his handsomeness and the warmth of his smile.

"I'm sorry to disturb you like this. I should have just knocked on the door, but I didn't want to disturb the household or—" He cleared his throat, not saying what they were both thinking. *Or face the wrath of your feud-fueling family again.*

The memory of the tower door slamming in Burke's face again and again as he pleaded with her father to let him marry her floated back to her mind. "I understand," she said quietly. "But what are you doing here?"

"You mean, what am I doing here *again*?" he said ruefully. "I…I want to apologize for yesterday. I wasn't planning on passing by Brora Tower, nor was I trying to…watch you."

His voice was strained, but its deep baritone sent shivers of memory through her. How could just his voice affect her so greatly, even after all this time?

"I was on my way back to Roslin, but I acted like a coward riding off like that."

"And tonight…?"

"I was sent by Laird Sinclair this morning with all haste. I am to discuss clan relations with your brother."

"But Ansel isn't here yet!"

His brow furrowed in confusion. "He isn't?"

"Nay, but he should arrive from Dunrobin tomorrow, or the next day at the latest."

An awkward silence stretched between them.

"I suppose…I should wait for his return…"

"Of course!" Meredith felt heat suffuse her face, and she cursed herself. She was being a terrible hostess, and moreover, she was acting like a moon-eyed girl. Burke had that effect on her—he always had. But she was a fool to think that she could go back to those dreamlike weeks when she and Burke had tasted first love. Time had passed. She was no wide-eyed, innocent lass anymore. She couldn't hope for things to simply return to how they used to be.

"I'll come down and let you in. We can have a room made up for you right away."

He hesitated. "I wouldn't want to put you out. The tower staff must have already retired for the evening. It is a pleasant night—I can just sleep in the open out here."

"Nay!" She clapped a hand over her mouth, hoping no one else heard her loud exclamation. "What I mean is, I wouldn't be a very good hostess while you wait for my brother if I didn't see that you have a bed to sleep in," she said in a lower voice.

His eyes sparkled in the light of the rising moon. "Perhaps we can compromise. I'll sleep in the barn tonight. That way, I won't disturb your household, but I'll be off the ground and under a roof."

If she had thought her face was hot before, it blazed now. Thankfully, it was dark enough that she doubted he could see her blushing. The memories of their time together in the barn came flooding back—their soft, innocent kisses, his strong but gentle hands on her waist, her hair, her back...

"I'll come down and see you settled," she said. Half of her regretted her offer, for it meant that she would truly be face to face with Burke again, and in their secret meeting spot, no less. Was she willing to risk the pain and shame if he had moved on from their youthful infatuation? What if...what if he were married to another?

But the other half of her had to risk it. She had to know once and for all if there was anything between them, or if there ever could be. She had survived Chisolm Sutherland. She could survive this.

She grabbed a cloak from the nearby armoire and slung it over her chemise, then slid on a pair of slippers. Then she lowered the old rope ladder out the window. Blessedly, she had never had to use the ladder for its intended purpose—retreating from a fire, or worse, escaping from invaders if they managed to infiltrate the tower. The stone walls of the tower house had never failed them—except to keep her in and Burke out.

As she descended to the last rung, she suddenly felt his warm, familiar hands around her waist. He helped her down the few extra feet to the ground, but his hands lingered for a moment. She turned in his grasp to face him.

His eyes were unreadable in the growing darkness, and she searched his face for clues as to what he thought. Impossibly, he was even more handsome now than he had been ten years ago. Though he had always been tall and broad-shouldered, he had filled out a bit since he was a lad of nineteen. Even covered in a white linen shirt, his muscular arms and chest were large and prominent. His jawline was more firm and defined, though it was just as smooth as she remembered.

After what felt like an eternity, he released his hold on her waist, and the loss of his touch was nearly painful. She gave herself a little shake, trying to clear her head.

"You remember the way, I'm sure."

"Oh aye," he said huskily.

She turned toward the barn, which stood several yards off from the tower. Behind her, she heard him take his horse's reins and walk the animal by his side. When she reached the barn, she drew back the door and entered, indicating an empty stall Burke could use for his horse.

As he took the saddle from the animal's back, she

stood nervously in the doorway, unsure if she should leave or not.

Thankfully, he saved her from having to awkwardly excuse herself. "I was sorry to hear of your father's passing all those years ago," he said quietly as he ran a hand down his horse's flank.

"Were you?" She should bite her tongue for such a sarcastic question, but she wouldn't lie and pretend. Not anymore.

"Aye," he said, straightening. "We had our...differences, but he wanted the best for you."

This time she did bite her tongue to keep from saying something unkind about her father, specifically regarding his choice of husband for her. Burke must not have noticed, for he went on.

"And I have just learned about the death of your...husband."

The last word came out a bit gruffer than the others. Could it still pain him that she had married another?

"I'm sorry for your loss. It must have been hard for you to lose someone you were so close to for so many years."

"What?" She couldn't help the startled exclamation that burst from her.

He brought his eyes from his horse to her. Though the barn was dim, the near-full moon rising outside slanted through the wooden boards, illuminating the confused look on his face.

"I just meant...to lose someone as dear as a spouse..."

So he had no idea of Chisolm's character or the nature of their marriage. She lowered her eyes to the straw-covered floor. "There was no love lost between my husband and me."

Suddenly he had closed the distance between them, and his dark gaze bore down on her. "Did he hurt you?"

"Nay, nothing like that," she said without thinking. But then she paused, looking back up into Burke's dark, concerned eyes. "He never hit me, but he was cruel and cold. He...hurt me in other ways."

"If the bastard wasn't already dead, I'd kill him myself," Burke said under his breath. Then his brow furrowed. "I'm sorry. I shouldn't speak ill of the dead, especially not about the husband of a...friend."

Her stomach flipped. "Is that what we were—what we are? Friends?"

Burke exhaled and rubbed the back of his neck with one hand. "Bloody hell, I'm a fool and a coward. I've danced around it long enough. I should just say what's on my mind."

A long second stretched and Meredith thought her chest would explode from the breath she was holding.

"Meredith, I never stopped loving you."

Burke's handsome face swam before her. Just before her knees gave out and her eyes filled with tears, he took the last step that stood between them and wrapped a steadying arm around her.

"Are you all right, lass?"

She felt like she couldn't breathe. Could this be happening? "I-I'm just so…"

His dark blue eyes searched her face, a crease in his brow marking his confusion and worry.

She took a deep breath and straightened her legs a bit. "I feel like I'm dreaming. Burke, I never stopped loving you either, even after all this time."

A flood of relief washed over his face. He kept his arm firmly wrapped around her to steady her, and he guided them both toward the back of the barn. "Can we speak more about this?"

She nodded, then giggled wildly, her excitement and lightheadedness mingling to make her feel once again like the seventeen year old girl who had been rescued by this strapping lad before her.

He stopped in front of the ladder to the hay loft where they used to talk and kiss for hours. She climbed the ladder with him close behind her. The scents of the summer evening air blended with the warm hay up in the loft. All was quiet except for the occasional snort or shift from the animals below.

Meredith settled herself in the hay next to Burke, her heart pounding. He took her hand in his, his thumb circling gently over her skin.

"I don't even know where to begin," he said with a nervous chuckle. "I suppose we should get reacquainted again."

She jumped straight to the question whose answer she feared most. "Are you not married, then?"

"Nay, I never married. The opportunity never really arose, but whenever I thought of it, it always seemed like…settling."

Her heart squeezed at that. "And what of the rest of your life?" The question seemed ridiculous, but she knew next to nothing about what had happened to him since the last time they had spoken.

He launched into tales of the battles he had fought alongside his cousins and the other Sinclair clansmen, of life at Roslin, and his most recent work for Robert the Bruce. At times he had her gasping in surprise and fear at the adventures he had lived through, and at others she had to clutch her sides from laughing so much. He had a way of lightening her spirits with his warm view of life.

After a particularly raucous tale involving a priest acting decidedly un-priestly when introduced to a barrel of Sinclair whisky, she held up her hands in surrender.

"Have mercy on me, sir," she gasped between giggles.

His beaming face slowly grew sober. "And what of you, Meredith? I know so little, only that your father and husband have died, and that your brother is away, to return tomorrow. But what has life been like for you these past ten years?"

The laughter died in her throat as she thought

about how to tell him about her life. Besides a few brief reprieves, her happiest memories had all occurred before her eighteenth birthday—and most involved Burke.

She decided that the truth was better than anything else. So she told him of her heartbreak at being forced to marry Chisolm Sutherland, and then the deeper, darker despair of coming to learn that her husband was cruel and uncaring. One by one, she had given up all the things she loved, so that a few years into her marriage, she barely left the tower to look for animals to sketch. She gave up dismissing the maids with whom her husband cavorted right under her nose, for he would simply take up with the next one. Toward the end of Chisolm's life, her days had been mostly solitary and silent.

While she spoke, Burke listened, grim-faced. Though he remained silent, he gave her hand a little squeeze every now and then.

"And now I am a widow," she said by way of wrapping up. "The least desirable sort of woman imaginable. I am no longer a maiden whose virginity can be leveraged into an alliance, and my father isn't here to make another advantageous match for me." She spoke matter-of-factly, as if she were talking about someone else's life. That's what it felt like. She had detached herself long ago as a means of self-preservation.

"You cannot truly believe that you are undesirable," Burke said, his eyes sliding over her. "You are more beautiful to me than when I first laid eyes on you."

"When you first laid eyes on me, I was nearly drowned and frozen solid!" she said, playfully tapping his wrist.

"Aye, and you were the most bonnie sight I had ever seen. That is, until I caught a glimpse of you yesterday." He raised her hand to his mouth and placed a soft, slow kiss between her knuckles. Even that simple act made her pulse hitch.

"I don't mean to sound sour," she went on, trying and failing to tear her eyes from Burke's lips. "Being a widow has allowed me to get back to my old self—or rather, to make a new self."

"That's a noble way of thinking of it. So, Meredith Sutherland, who are you now?"

She smiled faintly as she thought for a moment. "I still take joy in catching glimpses of the animals that live near the tower. I saw a linnet for what felt like the first time yesterday."

"Did you chase him like you did the fox?" His eyes shone with merriment.

"Nay, but I have many beastie-chasing days ahead of me yet," she replied with a faux glare. Then she went on more seriously. "I enjoy running the tower—really running it, I mean. I never got to be in charge of anything until Chisolm died. Now I can get things in order to my liking. And I enjoy the responsibility of the tower's service to the clan and to Dunrobin."

"What else?" he said softly, stroking the delicate skin on the inside of her wrist.

"I...I want to come alive in...other ways as well." Her voice nearly broke as she spoke the bold words. She wouldn't be ashamed, though. She wanted to know love again—emotionally and physically.

She watched as Burke's eyes darkened with desire. "I want that for you as well. I want you to feel loved, to *know* that you are loved, as you deserve."

She was at a loss for words, unsure of how to let Burke know what she felt for him. But he saved her once again from fumbling awkwardly for what to say, for in the next moment, he leaned in and took her mouth in a kiss.

Chapter Eight

His lips were soft and gentle at first as they brushed against hers. She leaned into him, longing to be completely enveloped by his strength, his clean, masculine scent, and his passion, which seemed to be boiling just below the surface.

He deepened and intensified their kiss, and in just seconds, she had crossed over into unknown territory. They had never kissed so passionately—the way a man kisses a woman, not the way a lad kisses a lass. Nor had she ever shared such emotionally intense contact with her late husband.

This was different. It was raw, filled with deep passion and hunger. He seemed to be communicating to her through his kiss, expressing all that had gone unspoken between them for ten years. She responded with her lips, silently conveying her longing, which seemed to have only intensified with time.

His tongue brushed hers, sending a bolt of sensation through her mouth and down her spine. Unsure of what to do at first, she let him lead, swirling their tongues together in a sensual rhythm. Tentatively, she met and matched his motions, which drew a soft groan from him. The sound reverberated through her lips, and the buzzing sensation caused her to shiver.

His hands slipped around her waist, under her cloak but above her chemise. His warm, large hands pulled her closer to him, so that their chests were pressed together. The feel of her breasts, covered only by the thin material of her chemise, rubbing against the hard planes of his chest brought a moan to her lips.

Without her awareness, her arms had risen and wrapped around his neck, holding him in their kiss. Her fingers dug into his muscular shoulders, hungry for more contact.

His hands moved from her waist to her back, and he gently massaged her as he held her to him.

"I have wanted this for so long," he whispered against her lips, breaking their kiss for a moment. "I have wanted *you*."

She responded wordlessly, squeezing his shoulders and bringing their mouths together once more.

His hands began to move from her back to her sides, right under her breasts. She suddenly felt needy, achy with a desire for his touch there. Sensing her longing, he slid both hands up slightly so that he cupped each breast.

His large hands felt incredible, but it wasn't enough. She wanted more sensation, more contact. Instinctively, she arched into his hands, creating more connection.

Just as he delved his tongue into her mouth in a penetrating kiss, he slid each thumb up to brush against the peaks of her breasts.

A jolt of liquid fire shot through her, and she gasped into his mouth. It was almost too much to take. Heat was gathering between her legs, and for the first time in her life, she dimly realized that her body was making itself ready for him, that she viscerally desired the promised contact waiting for her in Burke's embrace.

He continued to caress the peaks of her breasts, which had hardened into tight centers of pleasure, even as he teased and explored her mouth with his.

Suddenly, she couldn't stand not being able to touch his skin. Her fingers went to the tie at the neck of his shirt, and when the tie was loose, she let her fingertips brush the flesh of his upper chest. His muscles tensed under her fingers, and her stomach fluttered at the feel of the smooth steeliness of his body. He was battle-hewn and in his prime. She had never touched a man like that, all hard, lean muscle.

He dragged his hands from her breasts just long enough to tug the shirt over his head and toss it aside. Her eyes widened at the sight before her, illuminated in the moonbeams coming through the barn's wooden slats.

He looked like a pagan god. His light brown hair had come loose from its queue and settled around his wide, thickly muscled shoulders. His broad chest tapered to a trim waist, and she could see ridges of muscles defined by the shadows in the barn's low light. The faintest trail of hair led from his navel down to the top of his kilt, and presumably below.

Despite the fact that she knew what was beneath a man's kilt, she blushed, the heat warming her already sensitive skin. She met his eyes and realized that he had watched her raw appraisal of his body.

"Do I please you, Meredith?" he whispered huskily.

"Aye. And do I please you?"

His dark eyes seemed to glow, and he scorched her with a raw, heated look. His eyes moved to her lips, then to the open cloak and the ties at the neck of her chemise. Then his gaze slipped lower to her breasts. She glanced down and realized that their shape was easy to glean, and the dark tips were just barely visible through the material.

"Aye, you please me more than I ever thought possible."

She had been vaguely aware at one point many years ago that her face was pretty, and that her curves, slimmer but womanly nonetheless, were pleasing to men. But she had never felt so adored, so worshipped, as she did now with Burke.

"Kiss me again. And…touch me," she said, forcing herself not to lower her head with ladylike bashfulness. Instead, she meet Burke's eyes.

He obliged quicker than lightening. His hands once again sought her breasts, sending more flames of liquid pleasure through her limbs, as his mouth caressed and teased hers. She let her hands skim over his newly exposed skin, exploring all the hard planes and ridges.

Her fingertips found the trail of hair just below his navel and traced it downward. Burke shivered uncontrollably and made a sound like a half-formed curse against her mouth.

She broke off their kiss when her fingertips reached the belt buckle holding his kilt around his hips. She glanced down at the dark red material and her hand on his belt buckle.

"What is it, love?" he asked as she continued to stare in silence.

"It's just…your plaid…"

Realization dawned on him. "My *Sinclair* plaid."

She swallowed and met his eyes, trying to convey her pain and confusion to him.

"You think that you are dishonoring your clan and family?"

"I don't know. It has been drilled into me—into all Sutherlands—that the Sinclairs are our enemies, that they are—"

He smiled softly. "It's all right, lass. You won't offend me or tell me anything I haven't heard before from Sutherlands, the English, or any other number of foes."

The warmth in his eyes almost managed to chase away the sudden chill that was settling over her. "What if, even after all this time, my family rejects you? What if they send you away?"

His face grew serious. "Would you want them to?"

"Nay!"

"Do you think that what we are doing is wrong? Do you think that my love for you, and yours for me, is wrong?"

"Nay...but..."

He took her hand in his. "You're a widow now, remember? You are—how did you so elegantly put it?—'the most undesirable sort of woman imaginable.'" He couldn't help but chuckle, which drew a smile out of her.

"My point is, you are your own woman now, Meredith. As you said, you no longer need to look to your father, your husband, or even your brother for permission to do what is in your heart."

Something shifted inside her chest at his words. She was free, and yet she continued to doubt herself and look to others for approval. No more, she told herself firmly. The one thing she wanted, the one thing she had always wanted, was to be free to choose. She had that now. And she was making her choice.

"You're right," she said, locking eyes with him. "And I'll do what is in my heart." Without waiting for him to respond, she leaned in and pressed her lips against his.

Chapter Nine

There was no more hesitancy, no more fear, and no more doubt. Even as their tongues swirled together, she reached for his belt buckle, unfastening it.

The material of his kilt began unpleating and sliding from his hips, even though he was seated. He seemed to read the change in her, for his hands were suddenly everywhere at once—in her hair, on her breasts, around her waist, and molding to her hips.

He managed to push the cloak from her shoulders so that she was in nothing but her chemise. He leaned toward her until she tilted back into a soft mound of hay. The scent of it mingled with his exposed skin, making her feel wild and free.

"I have to see you," he mumbled against her mouth, then pulled back a little to undo the ties of her chemise.

Despite the warmth of the barn, she shivered as his fingers brushed the skin at her neck. He eased the chemise over her shoulders, and she shimmied to help him pull the material past her breasts, then her waist, then her hips. Finally, the thin garment slid past her feet and she was fully bare before him, splayed out on top of her cloak and the hay beneath it.

He inhaled sharply, and her eyes sought his, suddenly unsure and feeling exposed. But the look of raw hunger that lit his eyes made her forget any shred of embarrassment she might still cling to.

"You are the most beautiful woman I have ever seen," he breathed, his eyes roaming all over her, lingering on her dark hair spread behind her head, her breasts, her hips, and finally the juncture where her legs met.

Her eyes flitted down over him as well. He was on his knees above her, and his kilt had slipped into a pool around him on the loft's floor. Standing out from his body was his large, rigid manhood. She was no maiden, but still her lips parted in surprise at its size and length.

Before she could voice that surprise, though, he leaned back over her and placed a kiss on one of her taut nipples. She gasped and jerked as he flicked his tongue out to circle and tease first one nipple and then the other. By the time he leaned back on his heels again, she was writhing in almost unbearable pleasure.

He brushed his fingertips across her stomach and down her thighs, then wrapped his hands behind her knees and lifted slightly so that her legs bent. Then he let his fingers slide down the inside of her thighs, and, ever so slowly, he brushed the damp curls of her sex.

She gasped and moaned even though his touch was feather-light. Unconsciously, her legs fell open a bit, giving him more access to her. He slid a finger along her most sensitive flesh, and her body shuddered of its own volition.

Then he was positioning himself between her legs, but instead of his manhood, he lowered his head toward her most private place.

She suddenly stiffened. "What are you doing?"

"Has no one ever given you this pleasure?" he said, his eyes looking up at her but his head still lowered between her legs.

"Nay... What pleasure?"

Though his eyes were still fired with passion, he frowned slightly. "You deserved better, Meredith. Now let me give you all the enjoyment you've been robbed of all these years."

She didn't object, but she watched him warily as he lowered his mouth to the achy, damp spot between her legs. When his mouth touched her most sensitive spot, she jerked uncontrollably as a whole new kind of sensation washed over her. She let her head fall back onto her cloak and the mound of hay underneath as his mouth worked.

Wave after wave of deliciously torturous pleasure crashed around her as his tongue swirled and circled, delved and devoured her. She distantly registered that she was moaning and writhing wildly, but she didn't care. All she knew was that she never wanted it to stop. She never wanted to be anywhere but in Burke's hold, under his skillful hands and mouth.

The sensation hitched higher and higher, until she felt like she couldn't take it anymore, like she would explode.

And then she did.

Suddenly her pleasure burst into a thousand shards of light and she was soaring. Her body was light as air and throbbing everywhere. Then she was slowly spiraling back to earth. Burke's tongue lingered on her, sending reverberations echoing through her.

"I never knew…" Of course she knew that some women enjoyed the experience of lovemaking, but she had no idea that it could be like that.

She lifted her head to gaze down at him as he eased back from her and onto his heels. Suddenly her eyes were drawn back to his hard manhood jutting from his body, and a deeper, hungrier feeling stole over her.

He made a low noise in his throat at her bold perusal of his erection. She looked up into his eyes and saw her own simmering hunger mirrored back, except he looked to be starving.

"I want you, all the way, now, Burke," she breathed.

Like lightening he was over her, his hips between her legs. He leaned his weight on one elbow, and his other hand came between their bodies. She felt the brush of his swollen manhood against her still-tingling flesh, then his fingers glided over her. She inhaled sharply as the now-familiar pleasure returned to her in a heartbeat.

With another few strokes, she was panting and moaning once more. His fingers left her, to be replaced by the nudge of his manhood. He took himself in his hand, slowly guiding himself into her.

As he moved torturously, achingly slowly, her body took him in. He filled her deeply, until she cried out with the searing pleasure of his size. He pressed on until he filled her to the hilt. She arched, trying to take all of him in, longing to be closer and more bound to him.

Then he withdrew, but only partway. This time as he pressed back inside her, he rocked his hips, and she was treated to yet another new sensation. Once fully inside her, he ground against her, circling slightly.

She was vaguely aware that her fingernails were digging into the flesh of his shoulders, but he didn't seem to mind, or even register it.

He withdrew and entered again, this time faster. Soon he had built a torturous rhythm that had her arching and moaning, wordlessly begging him—for release and for more at the same time.

His jaw was clenched, and the muscles of his back strained under her hands. She realized that he fought for control, his pleasure was so great. That sent her own pleasure hitching higher. He seemed to sense that she was close to careening into the heavens once again, and he increased the pace, thrusting deeply into her.

It was her breaking point. Yet again, she reached toward the shattering paradise and found it, this time with Burke buried deep inside her. She felt herself spasm around him right before he jerked and cried out his release.

Their breath mingled as they both came back down to earth. He rolled slightly to the side so as not to crush her with his weight, but wrapped an arm around her and held her close to his naked body.

She was as limp as a milk-drunk puppy. Her whole body hummed with pleasure, and it wasn't just from their lovemaking. She managed to get her head onto his shoulder before complete and exhausted contentedness stole all her energy. Her last thought before sleep claimed her was that no matter what happened, she would never let Burke Sinclair go again.

Chapter Ten

Burke came awake slowly to a tickling under his nose. He inhaled and was rewarded with the scent of roses, but the tickle persisted. Cracking open his eyes, he found the source.

Meredith's head was tucked under his chin, her chestnut hair rolling in loose waves over her shoulders and his chest—and against his nose. He inhaled again, savoring her unique scent. She must use rose infused soap on her hair, he thought idly as he wound a dark lock around his index finger. But it was more than that. Something about her skin, her very essence, intoxicated him, claimed him.

She stirred, and he realized that a beam of morning sunshine had filtered through the barn's slats and now landed on her face.

"Good morning, love," he said, then kissed her hair.

"Say that again." She lifted her head so that she could look up at his face.

"Good morning?" he asked, intentionally innocent.

She pursed her lips and lowered her brow at him in

a mock frown, but it didn't have the desired effect of chastening him. Instead, he chuckled at her beautiful pout.

"Nay, you churl. The part about love," she said, cracking a smile.

Suddenly his desire to tease her vanished. "Good morning, *my love*. My Meredith."

Her dark brown eyes softened, and he felt his heart squeeze. In the morning light, he could see that she was indeed paler than she had been as a younger lass, and that the merry smattering of freckles that once sprinkled her nose had faded. But her cheeks were the rosy pink of a well-loved woman, and though her eyes held depths he still didn't understand, there was a contentedness in them now as well.

Suddenly she frowned. "I hope Beth hasn't come to my bedchamber yet this morning. My absence, along with the ladder being down, will send her into a panic."

She sat up, and the edge of her cloak, which he had pulled over her shoulder in the night, slipped down. The golden light of morning haloed her, softening her curves and making her skin glow.

He must have been gawking like a green lad, for she looked at his face quizzically, then glanced down at her naked body.

"Nay, don't be ashamed," he said quickly when she moved to cover herself. "You are so beautiful."

She smiled shyly at him, and if it were possible, he loved her even more at that moment. Now was the time to speak what had been in his heart for nearly ten years.

"Meredith, will you make me the happiest man on earth? Will you marry me?"

Her eyes widened and her lips fell apart slightly. He searched her face for a sign of her answer, and he saw both her deep love for him and her fears, likely for those who still might threaten to destroy their happiness.

She took a deep breath. Just as she was about to speak, the barn door was pulled back and sunshine flooded inside.

Meredith's breath turned into a gasp.

"What the devil?" a male voice said loudly from the doorway. Burke couldn't quite make him out, backlit as he was, but the man, drawing a horse behind him, could clearly see them in the loft at the back of the barn.

"Ansel!" Meredith said, shock and panic pinching her voice.

"Your brother?" Burke said to her as he fumbled in the hay for his kilt and belt.

"Aye, I'm her brother! Who the bloody hell are you?" the man bellowed, dropping the reins of his horse and striding into the barn.

"I am Burke Sinclair," he began in as calm a voice as he could muster as he fastened his kilt around his hips, "and I have come to—"

"*Sinclair?*" Burke's eyes had adjusted enough to see

the fury clearly written on the face of the man whose sister he had just slept with.

"Aye, and I have been sent—"

"You've been sent to dishonor my sister?" Ansel reached the base of the ladder leading up to the loft, and his hand gripped the great sword at his hip.

"I have been sent by Laird Sinclair to discuss a resolution of tensions between our clans," Burke went on levelly, though his teeth were beginning to clench.

"And you think the best way to open a peace talk is to bed my sister?"

"Ansel, please, hear us out!" Meredith said. She had quickly pulled her discarded chemise over her head, and covered herself further with her cloak.

Ansel rounded on her. "I left Dunrobin at first light this morning because I hoped to surprise you. Apparently I have succeeded all too well. How could you do this, Meredith? How could you sleep with a *Sinclair*?" His dark eyes narrowed. "How long has this been going on? Since before Chisolm died?"

Meredith gasped in horror at Ansel's words.

"You accuse me of dishonoring your sister, but perhaps it is you who disrespect her with your words," Burke said coldly. His words must have struck a chord, for a look of embarrassment flitted across Ansel's features.

"I haven't done anything wrong, Ansel," Meredith said, lifting her chin. "This is the man I love. I am going to marry him."

Burke's heart skipped a beat, and he looked to Meredith for confirmation of her words. Her eyes shifted to his, and his chest swelled at the love he saw in their dark depths.

"Like hell you are!" Ansel shouted, drawing his sword. "Come down here and meet my challenge for dishonoring my sister and my clan, *Sinclair*!"

Fear sliced through Burke's elation. It wasn't that he was afraid to fight. He completely trusted his skill with a sword. But the last thing he wanted to do was hurt Meredith's brother and dash all hopes of a reconciliation between their clans. He was under direct instructions from his Laird to pursue peace. And he would damn well never hurt Meredith by wounding her brother.

He slowly placed a foot on the top rung of the ladder and began easing himself down. He didn't bother to don any other clothes besides his kilt, hoping that his vulnerable state would cut through the fog of rage that enveloped Ansel.

"Let's talk this through, Ansel," he said carefully. "I don't want to fight you."

"Why? Are you so much of a coward that you would take my sister in a barn and then slink back to Sinclair lands without facing the consequences?"

Burke wouldn't take the angry man's bait. "I love her and I've asked her to marry me. I would much prefer to shake your hand as a brother than face you as an opponent." His feet reached the ground and he turned to face Ansel, raising his hands to show that he had no weapon.

"Fetch your sword and meet me like a man," Ansel bit out.

Burke slowly sidestepped to where Laoch stood quietly in a stall near the open door. When he reached his saddlebags, he tried to reason with Ansel once more. "It doesn't have to be this way, Ansel. There is no dishonor here."

Ansel merely spat and motioned toward Burke's saddlebags with the tip of his sword.

Reluctantly, Burke pulled the blade from his bags and faced Ansel. The man took several steps forward, forcing Burke to back out of the barn. Even as Ansel moved aggressively toward him, he kept the tip of his sword lowered. He would not be the one to start this fight.

Once they were out in the open, Ansel didn't waste any time. He raised his large sword and swung it down on Burke. It had begun.

Chapter Eleven

Burke blocked just quickly enough to prevent the blade from landing in the juncture between his shoulder and his neck. The force of Ansel's blow sent reverberations through his arms, though. The man was clearly a skilled fighter, and his anger likely fueled him.

Ansel recovered from the block quickly and swung again, this time at Burke's other side. Just as the blade was descending through the air, he heard Meredith's gasp from behind Ansel. He managed to block the blade once again, but the fraction of a second when his mind had been on Meredith cost him. He pushed Ansel's blade out of the way, but not quite enough. The sword caught his shoulder, slicing into his flesh and drawing blood.

He recovered and took several steps back, glancing down at his shoulder. "You've drawn my blood and defended Sutherland honor. Are you satisfied?"

"I'll not be satisfied until I see your body in the ground," Ansel breathed heatedly.

"Ansel, stop this madness!" Meredith pleaded from behind him. "I am going to marry him!"

Ansel kept his eyes on Burke, but spoke to his sister over his shoulder. "Father would disown you if he could hear you now."

Burke saw an opening for a new angle to reason with Ansel. "But Murray Sutherland can't hear her. He's dead."

Ansel's eye's narrowed, and with a wordless bellow, he charged. Burke just barely managed to block three mighty blows, all delivered in rapid succession, and all aimed to decapitate him. The sounds of their swords clanging together broke the otherwise quiet summer morning.

As Burke continued to parry and block, sidestep and duck, he became vaguely aware that the household staff of Brora Tower had come hurrying out to the sounds of clashing metal. A dozen or so sets of eyes now watched as Ansel continued to rain blows down on him.

"Your father is dead, Ansel," Burke panted, his arms growing heavy from the weight of his sword and the near-constant hail of strikes. He didn't quite sidestep fast enough, and Ansel's blade slid across his side. He vaguely registered the sting and the feel of blood flowing down his side. "This feud between us can die with him!"

Just as Ansel raised his sword for yet another attack, he paused, seeming to falter for a moment. Burke decided to take a chance and risk everything. He threw his sword down, to the gasps of surprise from those watching.

"Let us end this needless animosity between our clans," he said lowly. "Let it begin with my love for Meredith, and hers for me."

Uncertainty flickered across the other man's features. "It is my responsibility as my father's son to carry on his legacy and protect my family and clan."

"But is it really best for your family and clan to carry on a legacy of hate? I won't fight you, Ansel. Let us make peace."

Ansel's features hardened, and Burke feared he had made a fatal miscalculation. "He wasn't a perfect man, but he was my father. The Sutherlands and Sinclairs have been enemies for as long as anyone can remember. Now fight me!" He closed the distance between them like lightening, raising his sword to Burke's exposed neck. "Fight me!"

"Nay, brother!" Meredith screamed. She launched herself forward and between the two men so that she faced Ansel and shielded Burke with her body.

I will not lose him again.

"Meredith, get out of the way!" Ansel shouted at her, his fury and frustration evident on his face.

"Stay back, Meredith," Burke panted behind her.

"I won't, not until you listen to me, Ansel."

Her brother's chest rose and fell rapidly, the battle-lust still running in his veins. But his eyes, so much like hers, flickered to her for a moment. Slowly, he lowered the tip of his sword from Burke's neck.

She took a deep breath. "You are not our father, Ansel. You do not need to defend my honor, especially since there has been no wrong. But more importantly, you do not need to carry on with this feud just because Father wouldn't let it go."

"The Sinclairs have raided our lands for decades!"

"Aye, and Sutherland men have raided right back! How did it all start, though? Do you even know? Does anyone here remember?" she said, turning to the gathered household staff, who stood tensely nearby.

Ansel frowned. "It had to do with taxes. Many years ago, our ancestors raised taxes on Sinclairs who lived on Sutherland lands."

"The Sinclairs revolted and roasted the tax collector alive," Burke said from behind her.

"Then the Sutherlands were instructed by the King to restore order. They rounded up the revolters and burned them alive as retribution," Ansel finished, eying Burke warily. "The story goes that they even fed the charred remains to the dogs for good measure."

Meredith cringed at the gruesome history. "Haven't both clans' ancestors suffered enough? Haven't we *all* suffered enough under these never-ending hostilities?" She locked eyes with her brother, conveying to him without words the pain she endured now.

"I have always done my duty to Father and this family. Despite my pleas to be allowed to marry the man I loved—the man I still love—" she glanced over her shoulder at Burke, who was watching her closely, "—I obeyed Father and married Chisolm."

"The bastard," Ansel muttered, some of the heat coming back to his voice, but this time it was directed at her deceased husband rather than Burke.

"Now he's dead, along with our father, and yet those two men continue to rule our lives." She turned halfway toward Burke and took his hand. "This is the man I love, Ansel, and I will marry him. He is a good and honorable man, and I wish you could see that and give me your blessing." She steadied herself by looking into Burke's deep blue eyes. Then she spoke the words she feared to say yet knew in her heart to be true.

"But even if you don't give me your blessing, I will marry him anyway. I have given my life, my happiness, to Father's sense of duty. No more. You do not get a say in this, Ansel. I love you, but you will not decide this for me."

His dark eyes widened and he opened his mouth to object, but halted before the words came out. His gaze bore into her, searching her. She met his eyes unflinchingly, unafraid to show him just how serious she was.

Then he shifted his gaze to Burke, who stood at her side in front of him, hand in hand, bleeding and half-naked but resolute. Ansel's eyes lingered on the red Sinclair plaid belted around Burke's waist.

Meredith held her breath, fearing all was lost. But then he spoke, and his words shook her so deeply that her knees wobbled.

"You're right, Meredith." He dropped his sword into the grass at his feet. "Father thought he was doing what was best for you and the clan, and you have suffered for it. I think he knew only a few days after the wedding that he had made a mistake. But you were the one who had to live with the consequences. I...I only want what is best, and I don't want to fail the clan, but I *cannot* fail you again, as our father did."

Tears blurred Meredith's vision, but she could see that her brother was still chewing on something by the frown on his face.

"You spoke of peace, Sinclair. What did you have in mind?" Ansel asked, pinning Burke with a hard look.

"For starters, I'm going to marry Meredith," Burke said levelly.

"And you are doing so because you love her? Not because you are honor-bound to do so after I caught you with her in the barn?"

Burke smiled a little and gave her hand a squeeze. "She is the only woman I have ever loved, the only woman I will ever love. I am asking her to marry me freely."

"And you, Meredith? You want to wed this...man?"

"More than anything I have ever wanted before, brother."

Ansel narrowed his eyes at Burke again. "And what of our clans, of the raiding and trade embargos and hostilities?"

"If I understand correctly, you are close with your

cousin, Laird Kenneth Sutherland."

Ansel nodded in response.

"I am Laird Sinclair's right-hand man. Perhaps we can arrange a meeting between the two of them to discuss an end to the hostilities. We all fight for Robert the Bruce now—perhaps our alliance can also help the cause for independence."

Her brother nodded slowly. "That would be... good." The fires of battle were finally doused in him.

She let go of Burke's hand so that she could throw her arms around Ansel and hug him close as if they were children again. Though tears of joy choked her, she knew he would understand how much his actions meant to her.

"Beg pardon, milday, milord," Beth said from the crowd of gathered servants behind them. "Does this mean that we should prepare for a wedding celebration?"

Ansel broke their embrace and locked eyes with Meredith, waiting for her response. His silence and deference meant more to her than anything he could have spoken then.

She glanced back at Burke, who stood shirtless and bloodied, but whose eyes were lit with a deep and abiding love.

"Aye, Beth, we'll celebrate a week from today," she said through the lump in her throat. "It will be a union between not only two people, but two clans."

As the household staff filed back into the tower,

Meredith went to Burke's side once more.

"I've already waited ten years to marry you, and now you'll make me wait another week?" he said in a low, teasing whisper.

Ansel apparently overheard him, though. "Are you pressuring my sister already, Sinclair?"

"His name is Burke, brother," Meredith said with exasperation. Burke only chuckled.

Ansel grunted and picked up his sword from the ground, resheathing it. "Well, *Burke*, you fight fairly well—for a Sinclair, that is."

Burke raised an eyebrow at her brother. "Perhaps we can try again some time—on the practice field, of course." He extended his hand to Ansel, and after a brief hesitation, Ansel took his forearm in a firm shake.

Meredith blinked, trying to remember this moment forever. Her brother, a Sutherland, was shaking hands with the man she loved, a Sinclair. She had once thought that she was fated never to know happiness, never to truly feel alive and free. But as Burke wrapped a hand around her waist and leaned in for a kiss, she knew her life had finally begun, and all the happiness in the world awaited her.

Epilogue

There was a salty bite to the air as Burke emerged from the hatch door and onto the landing ringing Brora Tower's roof. Meredith turned toward him, her dark eyes filled with excitement.

"Look!" she said, pointing off toward the west. Burke's eyes followed the line of her finger. After a moment of searching, his eyes caught a flash of red fur cresting one of the distant ridges.

"He's back! But there aren't any ice-covered lochs for him to lure you toward." He wrapped his arms around her and pulled her back snugly against his chest so that they could both watch the fox. He also managed to pin her arms to her sides so that she couldn't swat him for his tease.

"You beast!" she squealed, halfheartedly struggling in his embrace. "Surely he isn't the same one as before." She managed to glance over her shoulder up into his face. "But it wouldn't be such a bad thing to be lured to a frozen loch if it meant that I could be rescued by a brave Highland warrior again."

He tickled her with one hand, drawing another

squeal and a giggle from her. "Only two months of marriage and you already want to trade me in for a newer, braver, brawnier rescuer, eh?"

She pleaded for mercy between gasps of air and peals of laughter. When she caught her breath again, she leaned back into his chest. "Nay, I suppose you'll do."

He almost launched another tickle attack for her saucy tone, but instead he squeezed her tighter and placed a kiss in her hair, which was rustling in the briny wind coming off the North Sea behind them.

"Perhaps you won't think me such a beast if I finally make good on the wedding present I promised you," he said, his eyes following the fox in the distance.

"I almost forgot!" She craned her neck again so that she could look up at him, a smile playing on her lips.

"Wait here," he said as he went to the ladder and descended to the chamber below.

Once he had the gift in his hand, he nearly bounded up the ladder again. He forced himself to stop once his head had poked through the hatch door to the roof. Meredith was waiting for him expectantly.

"Close your eyes," he said. When he was sure she couldn't see him, he emerged the rest of the way onto the roof, the gift in one hand.

"All right, open them."

Her dark eyes fluttered open and landed on his extended hand, in which he grasped several sheets of fine parchment.

The expectant smile on her face slipped, and her mouth fell open. "How on earth…?"

"Do you like it?"

"Do I…?"

His stomach twisted. Had he misjudged his present for her? "I thought you might use these to sketch animals. I know it's two months late for a wedding present…"

Her eyes finally shifted from the parchment in his hand to his eyes. "Burke…how did you know that this is the most perfect gift you could give me?"

Relief flooded him. "I can't take all the credit. Your brother told me a tale about a very naughty young lass who snuck into her father's study and covered his fine parchment with sketches of squirrels and eagles and the like."

Her face broke into a wide grin to match his own. Then she threw her arms around his neck, and he could feel her slim shoulders shaking with emotion. "Thank you," she whispered.

"You deserve a whole tower full of parchment, Meredith," he said into her hair. "This is just the beginning."

She pulled back, wiping her tears away, then rose up on her tiptoes to press a searing kiss to his lips.

"I was going to suggest that you get started using this parchment to sketch our friendly fox over there," he said against her mouth, "but now I think there is something else more pressing to attend to…"

She leaned into him, opening her mouth to deepen their kiss. Just as he was about to hurry them both down to their bedchamber, he heard the sound of hooves in the distance.

Meredith must have heard it too, for they both reluctantly pulled out of the kiss and turned toward the sound. A lone rider was coming in from the southeast.

She squinted. "I think that's Ansel."

Meredith's brother had been gracious enough to give them some privacy at Brora Tower after they were married. He had been spending most of his time at Dunrobin, which pleased Laird Sutherland as well.

Despite Ansel's initial hesitancy—and occasional open glares—he and Burke had slipped into a working relationship that Burke hoped could one day turn into brotherly regard. The turning point had been Burke's stroke of inspiration when it came to Brora Tower.

Meredith hadn't wanted to leave the tower after they were married. She had spent her whole life here, and finally felt like she was taking charge of the tower's upkeep. Burke hadn't objected (after getting Robert's blessing), but Ansel remained prickly about having a Sinclair under Brora's roof.

But even more importantly, Ansel was the one who had to convince Laird Sutherland to enter into peace talks with Laird Sinclair. To add to the challenge, Ansel also had to explain his sister's marriage to a Sinclair. Ansel had feared he didn't have enough to go on with his Laird.

Then Burke had proposed that Brora serve as not only the symbolic uniting of the two clans (through Meredith and his marriage), but also a strategic one as well. Brora Tower stood to the northwest of the Sutherland seat at Dunrobin, and not far from the border with Sinclair holdings. A signal fire lit on the tower's roof could not only be seen from Dunrobin, but also from Sinclair lands.

After some diplomatic meetings, Lairds Sutherland and Sinclair were able to come to an agreement that Brora would serve as a signaler of threats and invasions for both clans.

This arrangement went a long way in smoothing the tensions between not only the two clans, but also Burke and Ansel. But most important to Burke, it thrilled Meredith to have a delicate but growing peace between her husband and her family and clan. Ansel's visit from Dunrobin would hopefully bring more good news about the continuing peace talks between the two Lairds.

Burke followed Meredith down from the roof to the spiral staircase leading to the open room at the tower's base. A servant was just pulling open the tower's large door to Ansel when they reached the great room.

Meredith embraced her brother warmly and Burke exchanged a quick forearm grasp with him before they led him to a chair in front of the large hearth in the far wall. Now that it was early October, a marked chill hung in the air.

"What brings you to Brora, brother?" Meredith asked as Ansel held his hands in front of the fire.

"A letter, actually." He shifted his eyes to Burke. "For you."

Burke frowned. "From whom?"

"Laird Sinclair. He was just at Dunrobin for the latest round of peace talks. It seems that some of the farmers and crofters along the border between our lands continue to fight about which lands and sheep are whose."

Burke rolled his eyes. Peace was not the absence of war, but the constant state of actively avoiding it.

Ansel quirked a smile at Burke's annoyance. "They'll sort it out eventually, I'm sure." He handed Burke a folded missive with Robert's seal on it. Without waiting, Burke broke the seal and quickly read the message.

"What is it?" Meredith said, concern furrowing her brow. He must have been frowning at the contents of the letter.

"It's not bad," he said to reassure both her and himself. "In fact, much of it is good news. It seems that my cousin Garrick has gotten married to Lady Jossalyn Warren."

Meredith raised her eyebrows, a smile beginning to form. Burke had told her about Garrick and Jossalyn's connection, and how he had encouraged them to get married. "I hope I get to meet both of them soon."

"Aye, I hope so too. There's more, and it may throw us all together in the future. Apparently Robert the Bruce has a plan for my youngest cousin Daniel. The Bruce wants Daniel to secure his ancestral holdings in the southwest Lowlands through a marriage alliance. It looks as though there will be a fourth Sinclair wedding this year."

"Another wedding? Would we be able to go for the celebration?"

"Perhaps. I'm more worried that I'll be called to serve for less festive reasons."

"I heard something of that at Dunrobin," Ansel said, his face serious. "Our Lairds have been discussing more than just peace between our clans. The Bruce is gearing up to make a decisive move against the English now that Longshanks is dead."

"Aye, that's what the letter says as well," Burke replied. "I may be called to the Borderlands along with my cousins—and Sutherland men—if we are needed for a battle against the English."

Meredith's eyes widened and the color drained from her face. "You would both have to leave?"

Burke ran a soothing hand over her back. "Nothing's certain yet, love. Who knows, perhaps we'll just travel for Daniel's wedding celebration and that will be the end of it."

"But war is coming," Ansel said darkly. "And not just skirmishes and battles here and there. We must do something decisive if we are ever going to gain freedom from the English. The Bruce is ready, and so must we be, when it comes to that."

Meredith shivered at her brother's words. Burke longed to chase away her worries, but he feared that Ansel was all too accurate in his assessment. Edward II had yet to prove one way or another what his stance toward Scotland would be, but he could still take up the mantle of Hammer of the Scots from his dead father. The time was upon them to act.

For now, though, there was nothing to be done about all that. "Let us set such things aside for the time being," he said, looping his arm around Meredith's waist. She leaned into him, and he buried his nose in her rose-scented hair.

Now it was Ansel's turn to roll his eyes. "You two act more like lovesick bairns than a couple of married people. I'll stay for the afternoon meal, but then I'll head back to Dunrobin and leave the tower to you."

Meredith stuck her tongue out at her brother as he went to the kitchen to see about a meal for himself.

"He's right, you know," Burke said mock-seriously. "I can't seem to keep my hands off you."

"Nor I," she replied, a mischievous light in her brown eyes. "Even during the day my thoughts are filled with you."

He raised an eyebrow at her boldness. "So the fact that it is no longer forbidden for us to be together hasn't dulled your desire for me?"

She elbowed him playfully, then bit her lip to try to

stifle the grin that grew across her face. "Not in the least."

"Good, because we have a lifetime of loving ahead of us. We'd better not fall behind."

He took her hand and pulled her toward the stairs leading to their chamber, her thrilled laugher filling the air behind him.

The End

Author's Note

The Sinclairs and Sutherlands had several feuds dating back nearly one thousand years—almost as long as the two clans could be said to exist. Both clans seem to have committed atrocities against their hated neighbor. In the twelfth century, Sutherland churchmen had horseshoes nailed to their feet by Sinclairs and were forced to dance, and in return a group of Sinclair men were castrated to prevent them from creating any offspring.

I base the details of one of the long-standing feuds on a particular incident in the thirteenth century, almost one hundred years before my story takes place. Several Sinclairs started a rebellion in 1222 over steep tithes imposed by the Bishop of Caithness in Dornoch (on Sutherland lands). Unhappy about the tithes, the Sinclairs rioted, set the Bishop's cathedral on fire, and roasted the Bishop alive. The Sutherland Laird was charged with restoring order, so he gathered a force of Sutherland men and ravaged Sinclair land. Several towns, along with the Sinclair stronghold at the time, were completely razed. Eighty Sinclair men were tried for rioting, and four of the ringleaders were roasted alive, then fed to the town dogs.

Brora is indeed a town just north of Dunrobin Castle, but Brora Tower, which I locate more to the northwest and inland from Dunrobin, is fictitious. Tower houses were just beginning to be built when this story takes place, especially along the Borderlands, but also in mountainous or remote areas. They served the dual purpose of providing defensible structures in strategic locations, and also acted as fortified residences for the well-born. Smaller and less fortified than a castle, tower houses nevertheless protected against bands of attackers, and also served as watch towers that could signal impending danger (especially in the Borderlands). I am unaware of tower houses ever being shared by two clans, especially two feuding clans like the Sinclairs and Sutherlands, but it's a nice thought.

The parchment that Burke gives to Meredith at the end of the story probably would have been made from animal skins. Though paper mills were starting to appear in Europe in the fourteenth century, there likely weren't any in England until the fifteenth century, making paper rarer than parchment. Nevertheless, parchment was considered superior to paper at the time, because it was more durable and of a higher quality. Parchment was made by soaking an animal hide in lime, stretching it, scraping the hair off it, and cutting it to size. It would be a lucky person, indeed, who got to use such a valuable item.

Thank you!

Thank you for taking the time to read *Highlander's Return*! Consider sharing your enjoyment of this book (or any of my other books) with fellow readers by leaving a review on sites like Amazon and Goodreads.

I love connecting with readers! For book updates, news on future projects, pictures, newsletter sign-up, and more, visit my website at www.EmmaPrinceBooks.com.

You also can join me on Twitter at:
@EmmaPrinceBooks

Or keep up on Facebook at:
facebook.com/EmmaPrinceBooks.

Teasers for the Sinclair Brothers Trilogy

Go back to where it all began—with **HIGHLANDER'S RANSOM**, Book One of the Sinclair Brothers Trilogy. Available now on Amazon!

He was out for revenge…

Laird Robert Sinclair would stop at nothing to exact revenge on Lord Raef Warren, the English scoundrel who had brought war to his doorstep and razed his lands and people. Leaving his clan in the Highlands to conduct covert attacks in the Borderlands, Robert lives to be a thorn in Warren's side. So when he finds a beautiful English lass on her way to marry Warren, he whisks her away to the Highlands with a plan to ransom her back to her dastardly fiancé.

She would not be controlled…

Lady Alwin Hewett had no idea when she left her father's manor to marry a man she'd never met that she would instead be kidnapped by a Highland rogue out for vengeance. But she refuses to be a pawn in any man's game. So when she learns that Robert has had them secretly wed, she will stop at nothing to regain her freedom. But her heart may have other plans…

Garrick and Jossalyn's story unfolds in **HIGHLANDER'S REDEMPTION**, Book Two of the Sinclair Brothers Trilogy. Available now on Amazon!

He is on a mission…

Garrick Sinclair, an expert archer and Robert the Bruce's best mercenary, is sent on a covert operation to the Borderlands by his older brother, Laird Robert Sinclair. He never expects to meet the most beautiful woman he's ever seen—who turns out to be the sister of Raef Warren, his family's mortal enemy. Though he knows he shouldn't want her—and doesn't deserve her—can he resist the passion that ignites between them?

She longs for freedom…

Jossalyn Warren is desperate to escape her cruel brother and put her healing skills to use, and perhaps the handsome stranger with a dangerous look about him will be her ticket to a new life. She never imagines that she will be spirited away to Robert the Bruce's secret camp in the Highlands, yet more shocking is the lust the dark warrior stirs in her. But can she heal the invisible scars of a man who believes that he's no hero?

Follow the thrilling conclusion of the Sinclair Brothers Trilogy with **HIGHLANDER'S RECKONING**. Available now on Amazon!

He is forced to marry…
Daniel Sinclair is charged by Robert the Bruce to secure the King's ancestral holding in the Lowlands—and marry the daughter of the castle's keeper to secure a shaky alliance. But the lass's spirit matches her fiery hair, and Daniel quickly realizes that the King's "reward" is more than he bargained for.

She won't submit without a fight…
To protect her secret—and illegal—love of falconry, Rona Kennedy must keep her new husband at arm's length, no matter how much his commanding presence and sinfully handsome face make her knees tremble. But when an all-out war with Raef Warren, the Sinclair clan's greatest enemy, finally erupts, will their growing love be destroyed forever?

Teaser for Enthralled (Viking Lore, Book 1)

Step into the lush, daring world of the Vikings with **Enthralled (Viking Lore, Book 1)**!

He is bound by honor...
Eirik is eager to plunder the treasures of the fabled lands to the west in order to secure the future of his village. The one thing he swears never to do is claim possession over another human being. But when he journeys across the North Sea to raid the holy houses of Northumbria, he encounters a dark-haired beauty, Laurel, who stirs him like no other. When his cruel cousin tries to take Laurel for himself, Eirik breaks his oath in an attempt to protect her. He claims her as his thrall. But can he claim her heart, or will Laurel fall prey to the devious schemes of his enemies?

She has the heart of a warrior...

Life as an orphan at Whitby Abbey hasn't been easy, but Laurel refuses to be bested by the backbreaking work and lecherous advances she must endure. When Viking raiders storm the abbey and take her captive, her strength may finally fail her—especially when she must face her fear of water at every turn. But under Eirik's gentle protection, she discovers a deeper bravery within herself—and a yearning for her golden-haired captor that she shouldn't harbor. Torn between securing her freedom or giving herself to her Viking master, will fate decide for her—and rip them apart forever?

About the Author

Emma Prince is the Bestselling and Amazon All-Star Author of steamy historical romances jam-packed with adventure, conflict, and of course love!

Emma grew up in drizzly Seattle, but traded her rain boots for sunglasses when she and her husband moved to the eastern slopes of the Sierra Nevada. Emma spent several years in academia, both as a graduate student and an instructor of college-level English and Humanities courses. She always savored her "fun books"—normally historical romances—on breaks or vacations. But as she began looking for the next chapter in her life, she wondered if perhaps her passion could turn into a career. Ever since then, she's been reading and writing books that celebrate happily ever afters!

Visit Emma's website, www.EmmaPrinceBooks.com, for updates on new books, future projects, her newsletter sign-up, book extras, and more!

You can follow Emma on Twitter at:

@EmmaPrinceBooks

Or join her on Facebook at:

www.facebook.com/EmmaPrinceBooks

Made in the USA
Lexington, KY
30 January 2019